FROSTLANDS

FROSTLANDS

John Feffer

Haymarket Books
Chicago, Illinois

© 2018 John Feffer

Published in 2019 by
Haymarket Books
P.O. Box 180165
Chicago, IL 60618
773-583-7884
www.haymarketbooks.org
info@haymarketbooks.org

ISBN: 978-1-60846-504-0

Distributed to the trade in the US through Consortium Book Sales
and Distribution (www.cbsd.com) and internationally through
Ingram Publisher Services International (www.ingramcontent.com).

This book was published with the generous support of Lannan
Foundation and Wallace Action Fund.

Printed in the United States.

Library of Congress Cataloging-in-Publication data is available.

*For my brothers Jed and Andy, who taught me
to make the world a better place.*

Chapter One

I'm evaluating the signs of blight on the tomato plants in our greenhouse—a brief, head-clearing break from my research project—when my wristband pulses orange. I barely glance at it. I'm more worried about the tomato crop.

Orange alerts are not uncommon in Arcadia. It might be a lone wolf who sees the bright yellow solar paint on our silo and assumes our community is easy pickings. Or perhaps it's a band of survivalists in search of new digs. If we're lucky, it's just a computer glitch or an old, deaf buck that doesn't register the high-frequency signal the barrier emits. Orange means that the sensors on the outer perimeter wall have registered an attempted incursion. As soon as our wristbands change color, our defense corps begins its preparations, even though the automatic defenses almost always take care of trespassers. I'm no longer one of the regulars. I'm an excellent shot for an eighty-year-old, but I only shoulder a weapon these days for the annual deer cull.

The rest of the time I'm here in the greenhouses—or in the classroom or my lab.

The tomato blight is fungal—*Alternaria solani*. Untreated, it could substantially reduce yield. Fortunately, at this stage it's still containable. I'll need to adjust the ventilation to reduce the humidity, and we'll have to be more careful about the soil we use since we can no longer rely on a winter freeze to kill the spores. In the meantime, it's just a matter of removing the discolored leaves. I can deal with all three beds of Sun Golds and still have time to finish up in the lab before dinner. As the manager of Arcadia's greenhouses, I've conducted a low-intensity battle for more than a quarter-century against blights of all types. We've sustained some casualties along the way, but we're definitely winning the war. We have fresh vegetables all year long while the rest of the world has to put up with an unrelieved diet of seaweed.

Before I can set to work in earnest on the afflicted plants, though, my wristband pulses again. I look down, expecting it to fade to black. Instead, it turns red.

That gets my attention. I haven't seen a red alert in more than a dozen years. Red is serious indeed.

As quickly as my calcifying knees permit, I hurry out of the greenhouse and head for the inner perimeter wall, Section A, to take my assigned place. Thanks to the quarterly drills, I know exactly where to go, even though it's been a long time since the last red alert.

Fortunately, my knees don't have far to go. Section A

is a utility shed approximately fifty yards from the greenhouse. It looks harmless in its rundown state, the corrugated tin siding streaked with rust, the roof dented from a fierce hailstorm years ago. Housed inside is some supplemental farm equipment: a rototiller and plastic sheeting for the late-winter crop. Underneath a dusty hook rug, though, a trapdoor leads to a room containing much of Arcadia's computing power. This basement bunker is enclosed in enhanced concrete, protecting it from virtually all forms of conventional attack. Section A is one of the most important places in Arcadia, but we prefer not to call attention to it. Nothing sends a message of unimportance like an eighty-year-old sentinel.

Outside the shed, I'm greeted by Bertrand, glowing green.

He gives me a half-hug, his gun slung over one shoulder. "I'm hoping it's just a computer malfunction."

I fix my hair in a ponytail and select a weapon from the cache leaning against the shed's tin wall. To be candid, I can no longer operate heavier firearms. My capacities are winking out like stars in the night sky as the dawn approaches.

I ask Bertrand, "Do you know where the breach is?"

Red alert means the outer perimeter wall has been breached. If the red turns bright pink, someone's gotten through the inner perimeter as well. That's never happened, not since the initial wave of attacks nearly two decades ago. In the wake of worldwide crop failures in the late 2020s, those were what turned Arcadia from a peaceful intentional community into an armed compound.

Bertrand shakes his head. "Just the usual orders. Shoot anything that doesn't glow."

We take up our positions behind an earthwork that doubles as the side of a cistern for rainwater. The inner perimeter wall, invisible to anyone who isn't looking at just the right slice of the electromagnetic spectrum, runs through the center of that earthwork. We rest our guns on top of the adobe wall and stare into the distance. Beyond the water in the cistern lies flat, fallow land that will be seeded with spring barley in two months' time. The fields stretch to a stand of oaks that marks the outer perimeter. The barrels of our guns jut beyond the perimeter screen, as if we were on a parapet. Our inner wall is, in fact, a semipermeable membrane. Anything can pass through it from our side, nothing from the other. Nothing that we've encountered, at least.

Somewhere in the zone between the two invisible walls is an enemy. We don't know who or what it is. We don't know where it is. The lack of information is deliberate. We are supposed to focus on only one essential element: anything that doesn't glow.

We glow, Bertrand and I, as do all Arcadia members at the moment. When we go to red alert, our wristbands establish a personal perimeter, and the outlines of our bodies glow a phosphorescent green. We're not invincible. A direct hit by the latest generation of nanoweapon could probably do a great deal of damage. It's not something we want to test. We're expected to stay behind the perimeter unless absolutely necessary.

We're also not supposed to talk during our sentry time, but I need to know one more thing. "Where's Lizzie?" I ask him. She's supposed to be our third guard.

Bertrand doesn't even look at me. He's staring past the cistern's water as it ripples in the barely perceptible breeze of this early winter afternoon. "Reassigned."

"To?"

"Sector D."

That's all the information I need. The breach, I now know, is in Sector D.

Before I can properly process the implications of this, the field in front of us explodes in a frenzy of flying objects. They slice through the air above the fallow ground like a flock of swifts.

Bertrand is the first to start shooting, maneuvering his rifle expertly as if drawing a bead on targets at a firing range. I'm slower on the uptake, but soon my rifle's humming, too. I'm not quite sure what I'm trying to hit, though they look like compact metallic birds zipping twenty to thirty feet above the ground. All I know is that they're not green. They're not part of our defenses. It's happened so fast that it doesn't even occur to me that we shouldn't be shooting at all. Our automatic defense should be handling drones like these.

And then it's over, almost before it's begun. The field beyond the cistern is littered with shredded metal, sparkling like a crop of aluminum foil in the weak winter sunlight.

Suddenly the debris vanishes. Bertrand takes a surprised breath in.

I know instantly what's happened. I've read about these new delivery systems, which are solids only at extremely low temperatures. As soon as a remote kill switch is triggered, their previously shielded surfaces come in contact with the atmosphere, turn chemically unstable, and—sublimating from one state to another—transform into water vapor. If Bertrand and I were to venture onto the battleground, we would find nothing left of these polymers but a few drops of dew on the grass.

I look at him. He's no longer green. I glance at my watch. It has returned to its default shade of onyx.

"What was that?" Bertrand asks. Only now, after the emergency has passed, do I notice that his fingers are trembling.

"I don't know," I say. What I do know is that this was no conventional attack. The paramilitaries and survivalists in these parts have drones, but nothing like what we've just seen.

We stow our guns in the underground cache next to the shed. We know the drill. We must report to the Assembly Hall for a meeting in ten minutes.

Now that the adrenaline rush has subsided, I'm again feeling my age: the joint ache, the muscle strain, the fatigue. For an eighty-year-old, I'm in good shape. A four-decade regimen of weight training, yoga, aerobic exercise, and proper diet enables me to keep up with people twenty, even thirty years my junior. I'm not ready for what passes for retirement here in Arcadia.

Sometimes in the ecstasy of the moment, when I'm completely absorbed in my research, I forget my age altogether. All it takes, however, is a glance down at my hand, cracked and spotted like the outside of a baked potato, and I remember that I'm one bad fall, one hip fracture away from the downward slide that will make me a burden to the community. Arcadia doesn't have the luxury of expensive life-extending services. When the end comes, it comes swiftly, hastened by artificial means if necessary.

As we walk over to the Assembly Hall, I look at Bertrand's fingers. They're still trembling slightly as he runs a hand through his hair, and they come away slick with sweat. I'm surprised. Bertrand is a Capture, but from so long ago that most of the younger generation think he's an OM, one of the Original Members of Arcadia. Although he's been a quiet engineer during his time here, he was once one of the more militant members of the Quebec Wolves, participating in at least two raids on us before we captured him. He's no stranger to violence.

It's largely because of me that Bertrand is here in the first place. Though it's not something we've ever talked about, I suspect he knows it.

He came to us during the initial attacks of the early 2030s. In that hectic period, when our identity and very survival were at stake, Arcadia was divided into two camps—and me—when it came to dealing with the attackers we captured. The pacifists were pushing a policy of catch-and-release: expose the raider to Arcadia, then turn him or her out into the wilds with the gospel of our community. The realists preferred simple annihilation. The raids were, after all, taking their toll in energy expended and injuries sustained, and they argued for a brutal deterrence policy.

I was, as usual, an outlier. The pacifists were too naïve, I thought, while the realists offered a solution no better than the world outside. I proposed a third option. We would design systems to repel attacks. If confronted with a major breach, we would kill as necessary, but always capture one person, whom we'd deprogram, reeducate, and integrate into Arcadia. The Capture would become one of us. In this way, we would constantly test the strength of our community, diversify our gene pool, and send a message of strength through compassion to the outside world.

Having assimilated Bertrand, for instance, we encouraged him to contact his former colleagues in the Quebec Wolves. All attacks from that quarter soon ceased. Both the pacifists and the realists were mollified. We'd lost an enemy and gained an engineer.

As for Bertrand, he married the widow Morris and they soon had a daughter. His wife died two years ago from cancer. Their daughter Lizzie, only eighteen, has recently taken charge of our AI program, which also extends to the automated defenses. She's part of Arcadia's second generation, the whiz kids who give me some faint hope for the future. Bertrand, meanwhile, is so well integrated that he now serves on the Community Council.

"Are you okay?" I ask him.

He surreptitiously wipes his fingers on his pants. "It's been a long time since combat. Brings back some unpleasant memories. I just want a quiet life."

"That's all anyone wants."

I've often pondered the difficulty of being a Capture. When we were arguing over the policy, the realists insisted that, human nature being immutable, anyone we brought into the community would remain a potential rogue element. We could deprogram and reeducate all we wanted: at some deep level, the Captures would still harbor the urge to destroy us.

"If that's how we feel about Captures," I said at the time, "then we might as well pack up Arcadia and go our separate ways. Our community is based on the premise of change. If we can't change one person, how are we going to change the world?"

Some of the realists grumbled—deep down, they weren't interested in improving the world, just their chances of surviving in it—but in the end they went along with the majority. I have no idea if Bertrand knows about these debates. He's a recent addition to the Council. That gives him full access to the archives, but he may never have bothered to replay the relevant discussions. Still, I'm sure that he could sense, particularly in those early days, that some in the community expected him to revert to the man he'd once been. All along I've known that Bertrand's inner life is something else entirely. After what he's been through, because he has seen the wolf that hides inside Grandma's bedclothes, he is now the least likely person in Arcadia to take up arms against us.

The Assembly Hall is the only room in the community that can accommodate all 250 of us. When Bertrand and I arrive, it's already full and abuzz with speculation. Everyone is spooked by the disappearing drones. They don't understand how those weapons managed to penetrate the defenses in the first place. We take seats in the back. Before we can insert ourselves into the spiraling conjectures of our nearest seatmates, the two community co-chairs call the meeting to order.

Anuradha is the first to speak. "I know that all of you are very concerned about this red alert," she says in her rich, reassuring baritone. "We are still looking over the data records, but I think I can say with a fair degree of confidence that we've identified the digital breach and it won't happen again."

Slender in her orange sari, Anuradha cuts as striking a figure as she did when she helped found Arcadia as a young woman in 2022. Now she is in her late fifties, and the thick black hair that falls straight to her shoulders is threaded with gray. She's confessed to me several times during our evening constitutionals that she's tired of the burdens of leadership. This is her fifth rotation as co-chair and she wants it to be her last. I can sympathize. I also did five terms as co-chair, and it is a taxing job. In theory, I'm happy for Original Members like Anuradha and me to turn over the keys to the next generation. In practice, I have a few reservations. Which is why I've been urging her to stay on for a sixth term, even if it means she won't be able to focus on her primary job of livestock management.

The other co-chair, Zoltan, a platinum-haired young man a head shorter than Anuradha, clears his throat as he always does when he's nervous and preparing to speak. He is serving his first term. He was born and raised in Arcadia, so he knows nothing but this small world of ours, which makes him parochial in his tastes. Such narrowness of focus, however, can be useful. When it comes to the world of computers, he is brilliant, maybe even a genius.

"The breach lasted for no more than ten seconds," Zoltan says in his high-pitched, breathy voice. "We are now fully back in control."

"But who was it?" asks someone I can't see in the front row, and suddenly the audience is again murmuring.

Anuradha puts up a hand and waits patiently for the noise to subside. "We're not sure yet. But we should have a good idea by the end of the day. The most important thing is: we don't expect any more attacks in the near future. We handled this one very effectively, which sent a strong deterrent message to whoever launched it."

"We'll need a cleanup crew for Section D," Zoltan adds. "Some of the outer buildings in that quadrant sustained minor damage. And we'll need the forest maintenance team there as well."

Bertrand speaks up. "The drones. They disappeared. How did that happen?"

"A sublime polymer," Zoltan says. "We did manage to prevent one of them from dissolving, though. We'll see if we can identify its chemical signature and then trace it back to its owner."

I'm intrigued. I raise my hand to ask about the drones. "How on earth did you manage to—"

Zoltan speaks over me. "If anyone experienced any equipment malfunctions, please come up to us and report."

"For dinner tonight, the cooks will prepare something special from our latest deer cull," Anuradha adds. "And I think this would be a good occasion to test the first batch of apple brandy."

A few routine explanations, plus the prospect of a filling dinner and an evening of drinking, have calmed everyone's anxieties. They don't satisfy me, though. When I find Lizzie, I'll get the real story of what happened in Section D.

I'm on my way out the door when Zoltan suddenly appears in front of me. "Hey there, Rachel, you're looking for Lizzie, aren't you?"

Zoltan is like that. He has an uncanny knack for knowing what's on your mind. It's no surprise that he can beat all the humans in Arcadia at chess.

"Bertrand and I expected her, so..."

"Right now she's in quarantine."

"Did something happen?" I ask, instantly worried.

"She's fine," Zoltan says smoothly. "But I want you to

join her there."

Zoltan has taken to his co-chair position with the ease of a born politician. He likes moving all of us around Arcadia as if we were so many chess pieces. The problem is, I can't figure out his motivation. I've never been sure whether his political instincts are the sign of a bona fide leader or a master manipulator. Before his parents left Arcadia, he was just a sweet wunderkind. Afterward, a darker note crept in.

I said I had reservations about the next generation of leadership. I should have been more specific: my reservations are all about Zoltan.

I try to stay one step ahead of him. "You want me to look at this drone you collected."

Zoltan shakes his head. "Lopez and Winterson are already taking it apart."

I'm miffed. I know more about chemical engineering than either of them. "Then why do you want me in quarantine?"

"Anuradha and I agree that it would be useful to have an OM in on this from the start. Anuradha suggested you."

"In on what?"

Zoltan steps closer to speak in a lower tone. "We have another Capture."

Chapter Two

Once upon a time I testified before the great assembly of our land.

When I describe this event to our children here in Arcadia, it sounds like a fairy tale. Once upon a time this old woman was a young idealist who tried to persuade our mighty Congress that a monster was stalking the land.

"Did they listen to you, Auntie Rachel?" the children ask.

"Oh, they listened to me, but they didn't hear me."

"So what did you do?"

"I thought and I thought, and I wrote and I wrote, and I put together an even better presentation," I say patiently. "I had to somehow describe the monster in a way that these mighty people could understand it."

"What did the monster look like?"

"It was invisible, my dear children, but we could feel its hot breath and see the terrible things it did. It could make the oceans rise. It could make the crops wilt in the fields. Still, we kept feeding this terrible beast."

"But why?"

"It's what the monster demanded. Some monsters want to devour little children. Others insist on young maidens. But this monster demanded tankers of oil and truckloads of coal. Even as it grew, it demanded more and more."

The children are wide-eyed by now. "What did you do?"

"I talked to those great people again and tried even harder to describe the monster." As I slip into the past, the faces of the children become those of long-dead politicians. "I provided more detailed graphs of rising temperatures. I cited statistics on the impact of burning coal and oil and natural gas. I displayed photos of what the melting ice and the surging sea had already done. And then I showed them the future: submerged cities, drought-stricken lands, dead seas. They looked, but they didn't see. They listened, but they didn't hear."

Exclamations of concern jolt me back to the present. I gaze at my little students. They are simultaneously confused and upset.

"Great people are not always good people," I conclude.

"What did you do then, Auntie Rachel?"

"I stopped talking, my darlings. I came here to escape the monster. I came to Arcadia."

They look disappointed. The children know their fairy tales. They expect someone—a knight in shining armor, an orphan child with special powers—to appear suddenly and slay the monster.

"There was no knight," I lament. "The monster still lives. We can feel its hot breath even today."

"It's not fair," complains a little boy. "You should have killed it."

"Why didn't our grandparents run the factories every *other* day?" a bright young girl pipes up. "Why didn't they drive those stupid cars just on the weekend?"

"Ah, my dears, it was our failure, the failure of the international community."

Our children know nothing but Arcadia and our fully sustainable life here. What we don't grow, we synthesize or produce on our 3D printers. We conduct limited trade with nearby communities. If there's an unexpected death, we issue an extra birth permit. If our solar batteries run low during the winter, we ration energy. Everything is reused or recycled, from our chicken bones to our night soil. The children of Arcadia don't understand waste any more than my generation could have comprehended slave labor. It lies beyond their moral universe.

They also don't understand the antique notion of an international community. They've never ventured beyond the walls of Arcadia—they don't get their travel permits until they're eighteen—so it's only thanks to virtual tourism that they've seen anything of the world outside. And what they've observed on their VR jaunts only reinforces their desire to remain here. Today, the world is a collection of sharp little shards, what my ex-husband used to call the

Splinterlands. My students can't grasp how these shards once fit together to form larger nations that, in turn, cooperated to tackle common problems like climate change. It reminds me of that old story of the elephant and the blind men. The children of Arcadia can understand the parts; it's the whole that eludes them, because there is no whole any more. The elephant's been carved up like a holiday roast.

Think of the international community as a human being, I tell them. In 1945, it was a squalling infant born to bickering parents. A troubled childhood was followed by an awkward youth. Only in middle age, with the end of the Cold War in 1989, did it finally thrive, a period that ended abruptly in the new century when it progressed prematurely into its dotage. In 2020, at seventy-five years old, the international community was past retirement age, frail of health, and in desperate need of assisted care.

This aged body, this Knight of the Sad Countenance, was supposed to be our savior, the slayer of the horrible monster. Unfortunately, it could barely lift a lance.

Without some knowledge of the life cycle of the international community, my students can't possibly understand why global temperatures continued to rise in the first part of this century, despite the best efforts of scientists, environmentalists, and concerned citizens. Several small countries—Uruguay, Bhutan—went to extraordinary lengths to reduce their carbon emissions, and more than a dozen cities eventually became carbon neutral. Individuals adopted vegetarianism, drove electric cars, turned down their thermostats in the winter—as if lifestyle changes alone could slay the monster.

A global problem, however, required a global response. A treaty signed in Paris at the end of 2015 attempted to keep temperatures from rising two degrees Celsius over the preindustrial average. I told our mighty Congress that it wasn't enough. In a clear indication of just how highly they considered my opinion, these political grandees ignored what I had to say and, like a community of addicts, continued to seek out their drug of choice offshore, under Alaskan snowfields, and in the frackable shale substrates of the heartland.

Led backward by the United States, which announced in 2017 that it would withdraw from the Paris agreement, the international community abandoned all hope of sustainability and embraced instead its lesser cousin, resilience. I try to explain to my children that sustainability is all about harmony—maintaining balance, never taking more than what we give back. Resilience, on the other hand, is about making the adaptations required by a crisis. The judgment of Paris, with its nod toward resilience, was an acknowledgment of failure. Global temperatures crossed the two-degree mark in 2034, decades ahead of schedule. By that time several small Pacific islands were already gone and millions of climate refugees were pushing further inland from their flooded coastal homes. Still, today, the waters rise.

"But we have to do something!" the children cry.

"We are doing something," I reassure them. "Every

day that we live here in Arcadia, we send a message to that dragon. We send a message that we will not be defeated."

I provide them this reassurance but refuse to give them false hopes. I could tell them about my research project, about how close I am to cracking the mystery of the ice-albedo feedback loop. But it might hit an unexpected snag. Or we might not be able to persuade what remains of the international community of scientists to back the program. Or I might be carried away suddenly in my sleep by a heart attack.

In any case, almost no one in Arcadia knows about my project. They think I'm just an elderly ex-scientist who potters around without purpose in her laboratory. Good old Rachel, they whisper to each other, it's nice that she keeps her mind active. But maybe, instead of using up our precious resources to keep up that laboratory of hers, she should just do crossword puzzles and leave science to nimbler minds. They're more interested in the immediate applications of science, like squeezing extra energy from our solar paint.

We Arcadians are acutely aware of the dangers of climate change. But, like most people who haven't been submerged by coastal waters or swept up in the latest superstorm, we've become inured to the urgency of the situation. Our human brains are structured to focus on the short term—on getting through the day.

But I'm a scientist. I take the long view. And the long view is not reassuring. Consider the graptolite.

Graptolites were tiny sea creatures that once lived in

colonies huddled at the bottom of the ocean. Other graptolites floated like ribbons of seaweed on the water's surface.
They looked like jellyfish from Mars, with their bulbous
heads and dangling, hairy dendrites. For nearly 200 million years, they prospered in their aquatic world. They
probably thought—if they thought at all—that such longevity guaranteed them eternal life on this planet. Then
came the Carboniferous Period and a brief but severe ice
age. Goodbye, poor graptolites, along with 86 percent of all
other species. It was just one of several purges to which the
earth has submitted.

Before evolution culminated in mankind, its most glorious and destructive creation, the planet witnessed five
episodes of mass extinction. The most devastating came at
the end of the Permian era, around 250 million years ago,
when 96 percent of all marine species and 70 percent of
all land animals died out because a huge volcano exploded
in present-day Siberia and set off a chain reaction that radically raised the temperature of the seas. All those long-gone
creatures left behind no more than a few marks on stone
and some petrocarbon pools beneath the earth's surface.
Compared to the Permian event, the Carboniferous extinction that knocked off the graptolites was a relatively minor
apocalypse.

But not for the graptolites.

"Who cares about those stupid animals?" says one of my
low-performing students.

"Exactly," I respond. "And who ultimately cares about

us and what we leave behind?"

They have no answer.

I once studied ice. I traveled to the polar extremes to extract frozen columns of water from the ground in an attempt to understand more about our own era of global warming. This work accustomed me to think geologically, to consider the grand sweep of human history as the merest sliver in the planet's 4.6-billion-year timeline. The earth has repeatedly warmed and cooled in a set of protracted mood swings that has encompassed the epochs. Many species have died out thanks to spectacular events, like an asteroid crashing to earth or a massive volcanic eruption. But no wrathful god or malevolent alien force has proven necessary for human beings: we're quite capable of being our own worst cataclysm.

At first, we just scratched at the ground, altered the landscape, replaced majestic trees with quotidian corn. Eventually we discovered the great gift that the graptolites and the giant ferns and the mighty dinosaurs left us—themselves, turned carbon beneath the ground. In an instant of geologic time, we heedlessly burned through our natural resources while creating weapons of mass destruction capable of doing in the world hundreds of times over. We flirted with the option of going out with a bang but now seem determined, like the proverbial frog in a pot, to go out with a whimper of heat exhaustion.

The easiest way for the earth to regulate itself during this moment of increasing disequilibrium would be to cast off its most troublesome creatures. We're like the bad guests who continue to overstay our welcome: no matter how many hints we get from the hostess, we just keep eating and drinking and bloviating. Meanwhile, the planet checks its watch and wonders when it can safely declare "Time!" and shoo us out the door.

We could have turned things around in the 2010s. Instead, in one country after another, we elected the least capable people to navigate our way out of treacherous waters. Nowhere was this more obvious than in the once-United States. The election of Donald Trump in 2016 proved such a disaster that a chastened nation, instead of christening public buildings after him when he left office, bestowed his name on the devastating, climate-change-energized hurricane that struck the East Coast in 2022, causing billions of dollars of damage. Like its namesake, Hurricane Donald began as a squall, only later developing enough force to destroy the national capital.

My husband and I lost our home in Hurricane Donald. Having never liked Washington, I was happy enough to leave the city to the floodwaters. That's when I also decided to slough off my previous life as if it were little more than a sheet of dead skin. I divorced Julian and reverted to Rachel Leopold, the name I'd been using only for my scientific publications. And I retreated to Vermont where an old friend, Anuradha Shiva, was starting an experiment in sustainable living.

Here in our community of Arcadia, I've cultivated our

gardens and watched the inexorable rise of the global thermometer ever since. We have a good library, a real one, assembled from the basements and attics of farmhouses in the area. No one reads books anymore, not the paper versions at least, so we had our pick. What did Cicero say? If you have a garden and a library, you have everything you need. Well, almost. These days you need a good semiautomatic as well. In addition to overseeing the greenhouses, I teach science in our school. And I work on my pet project, the culmination of my six decades as a glaciologist.

In this Vermont community where I've lived for the past quarter-century, I no longer take ice core samples. There isn't much point (or much ice left, either). Instead I focus, with the urgency of the condemned, on my project. Meanwhile, we survive as best we can while bracing for yet another tempo shift that will force us to measure our lives not in decades but in years, or even days.

Here's how I try to explain this to my students.

"Imagine that you are a healthy and happy ten-year-old looking forward to many decades of love and life. Then, one terrible day, a doctor tells you that you have cancer, stage four. Fatal. You had been measuring the future in decades. Suddenly those decades disappear, leaving you with only a few years to go. Your parents, skeptical about vaccinating you as a baby, now reject conventional cancer treatments. First they deny the diagnosis outright. Then they urge you to eat ground-up apricot pits, drink special teas, and go on a high-fat diet. Nothing works, and the years turn into months, and those months into days, as the world closes in."

"Now," I go on, "substitute 'human race' for 'ten-year-old' and 'climate change' for 'cancer.' Do you see the problem?"

Some of the more sensitive students begin to cry. Their parents will complain to me, but I won't listen. That's one good thing about being eighty years old. You can get away with a lot—and when you don't get away with it, you don't care. I tell the parents that we have to toughen up their children, not just with work in the fields but here in the classroom as well. They'll need mental fortitude to survive the existential traumas that await them.

"We all have cancer?" a young boy asks in a quavering voice.

"Shush, that's not what she's saying," his classmate whispers to him.

But of course the tearful student is right. We all have cancer. In that pivotal year of 2016, we'd already received a poor diagnosis. The election of Donald Trump was our way, as a country, of first denying the problem, then refusing medical treatment, and finally embracing one quack remedy after another. I dearly hope that Arcadia doesn't turn out to be a hospice facility.

In the aftermath of that election, I struggled with the contraction of time and space. As geologic time shifted into human time, the map of my world shrank while the international community crumbled into ever smaller pieces.

During the first part of my adult life, I imagined myself part of a global fraternity of scientists. Then I worked at a national level to save my country. Here in Vermont, I've ended up confined to a small plot of land: an intentional community that's walled itself off from an increasingly dangerous and hostile world. Soon enough, I'll find myself in an even smaller space—underneath the rosebushes. Thus does the world close in on us.

We're still doing fine here in Arcadia. Climate change has turned northern Vermont into a farming paradise, and our citrus crop was excellent this year. No federal government interferes with our liberal community guidelines. We have enough guns to defend ourselves against outside aggressors. Everything that's killed the larger community beyond our walls has only made us stronger. So far.

Perhaps, like the monasteries of the Middle Ages, communities like ours will preserve knowledge until the distant day when we exit this era of ignorance and pain. Or perhaps, like the graptolites, we'll fade away and evolution will produce another species without the flawed operating system that doomed us. The graptolites were mute. We humans can speak and write and film ourselves in glorious 3D. These skills haven't saved us, but our ability to document our times—as I am now documenting mine—will perhaps save someone, someday, somewhere. Everyone prefers a happy ending to a tearjerker. With these documents, these core samples of our era, perhaps we can still somehow save the future.

"Tell us what to do," my charges implore me. They are still of an age when everything seems possible and the future looks friendly, not armed and dangerous. I'm probably the first person to tell them otherwise.

I can fill them in about the past, but I can't tell them what to do. I barely know what to do myself.

The ice, all the precious ice that I once studied, has nearly disappeared, and with it the ability of the earth to reflect the sun's rays. Unprotected by the ice and snow, the ocean waters absorb more and more of the sun's heat, growing warmer still. This is the ice-albedo feedback loop. Yet a greater catastrophe lies just around the corner: huge amounts of methane are trapped beneath the remaining Arctic permafrost. If this gas is released, then it's game over.

So, that is my project—to preserve and regenerate the permafrost before it's too late. I'm close to a solution. I just need a little more of that most precious commodity for an eighty-year-old.

Time.

Chapter Three

Lizzie looks tired—and scared. Her pale face is even more bloodless than usual.

I'm not sure why. Today's attack was short and the damage limited. Neither Anuradha nor Zoltan seemed particularly worried about the breach or its consequences, but Lizzie looks as though she's seen a ghost.

The Capture is no ghost, though. She looks very solid indeed, sitting on a chair in the Quarantine Room, safe behind protective glass. She's a young woman with startlingly blue eyes and smooth ebony skin, and she's gazing about the room with mild curiosity. She doesn't look dangerous in the least. Thanks to the Quarantine Room, any murderous diseases lurking in her bloodstream or murderous plans lodged in her psyche can't possibly harm us. The room has, in fact, prevented a succession of plagues from reaching our community—the avian flu in 2033, last year's PNC3 staph infection—not to mention a suicide bomber who blew himself up a dozen years ago and, other than traumatizing Lizzie's predecessor, did no damage.

Skipping the social niceties, as is her style, Lizzie gestures in the direction of the Capture and says, "Watch this."

She makes a movement on a screen in front of her that releases a microdrone from an aperture in the far corner of the room just behind the Capture's back. It speeds directly at her dark, shaven head, sharp beak aimed at the base of her skull. I'm tempted to turn away before metal strikes bone. But the Capture just casually tilts her head to one side at the last moment and plucks the metal object from the air. She looks at the deadly projectile without curiosity and then slowly crushes it as if it were an errant hornet.

"You get it?" Lizzie says.

I'm startled, but yes, I understand. I'd expected flesh and blood, another Bertrand. I manage to ask, "Why is she still here?"

"I disabled the kill switch," Lizzie explains. "It wasn't easy. There were ten of her. She was the only one we preserved."

"Also a sublime polymer?"

"No, a conventional kill switch. The other nine just combusted before I could freeze them and hack into their systems."

"She looks sophisticated."

"The most sophisticated I've ever seen. That's what worries me. Where does she come from, Rachel?"

I have my suspicions. Instead of voicing them, I ask

Lizzie, "Are there any bugs?"

"Oh, she has bugs. Listen." Lizzie makes another movement on the screen and then speaks a little louder. "What is my name?"

The Capture looks bewildered. "Your name?"

"What's my name?" Lizzie repeats.

The Capture suddenly slaps her palm against her forehead. Her head recoils from the blow. Once. Twice. Three times. It's painful to watch.

"Okay, stop," Lizzie says. "My name is Lizzie."

The Capture stops and smiles in the direction of Lizzie's voice. "Hello, Lizzie."

Lizzie turns to me. "She does that whenever she doesn't know the answer to a direct question."

I can't help but laugh. "I wish some of the men in Arcadia had that flaw!"

"I'm sure she has other bugs, but that's what I've found so far." Lizzie flicks her black bangs away from her eyes. "They didn't spend a lot of time programming her to interact with humans in real time. She's a Spongebot. Absorb and transmit. I've disabled the transmit function."

"We should introduce her to Rupert, perhaps they'd get along. As long as he doesn't ask her any unanswerable questions."

"He might have a better shot at determining where she comes from," she admits.

"You've tried asking her, I imagine. Or does that produce more head-thumping?"

Instead of answering me, Lizzie again speaks to the Capture. "Where do you come from, Karyn?"

"I was born in Canton, Ohio," she replies.

"And who do you work for?"

"I'm self-employed. I do some spot welding to make ends meet. But I spend most of my time creating graphic novels."

"And what brought you here to Arcadia?"

"I was hiking and got lost."

"Actually, you were part of an armed raid on this community," Lizzie points out matter-of-factly.

Karyn is not taken aback by this information. "I must have accidentally fallen in with a bad crowd."

"You also were armed."

"Was I?" Karyn looks genuinely perplexed. "I don't remember that."

Lizzie turns off the mic. "There's a lot she doesn't remember. If it were up to me, I'd turn her into parts. She makes me uncomfortable."

Lizzie is like that: unsentimental. Sometimes I think that Rupert, our own AI, has more of an emotional life than she does.

I look at Karyn, with her smooth bald head and the Gothic tattoos running up and down her neck. "I suspect that she's going to be worth more than the sum of her parts. You've scanned her code?"

"It's clean," Lizzie says. "Whoever designed her knew how to wipe away the fingerprints."

"We could incorporate her into the community. She's harmless now that she's disconnected, right? We could use a good spot welder. If they bothered to program that into her."

Lizzie brings up a screen of unintelligible strings of characters. "I've machine-scanned her code very carefully. But there might be a Trojan in there that I don't recognize. I don't want to be responsible for the people she strangles in the middle of the night. Look at what she does to her own forehead."

"I don't think she's designed to kill anyone."

"You believe she's just a harmless graphic novelist?"

"You said there were ten of them, right? Can you show me the schematic of the attack?"

Lizzie pulls up 3D archive footage of Arcadia, rewinds it to just before the attack began, and hits play.

It's a fully automated assault. First comes some kind of pulse that briefly brings down one segment of the outer perimeter. After a couple minutes, the drones discover the opening and pour through like bats from a fireplace. They quickly circle the outer ring. Karyn and one other AI follow through the breach before the virtual wall repairs itself. The others remain arrayed in a circle around Arcadia. Then, with the exception of Karyn, all the intruders disappear, either as a result of our firepower or their own auto-destruction. Karyn is the last bot standing. I look at the time signature. The outer perimeter was down for less than ten seconds, and the whole assault lasted no more than ten minutes.

"They didn't even try to penetrate the inner perimeter," I point out. "This was just reconnaissance. How much information did they send back before they were destroyed?"

Lizzie shows me the figure. It's staggering.

"How did they disable the outside perimeter?" I ask her.

"I don't know." She swallows. She's not accustomed to the fog of ignorance.

"It's not your fault, Lizzie. Whoever it was probably has the best coders in the world working for them. Look at Karyn. This is no random army of hackers."

Lizzie manages a tight smile. "Do you want to bring Rupert over?"

"Sure. Plus some scrap metal and some pens and paper. Let's see how talented our new Capture really is."

I find Rupert sitting in his favorite location, a corner of the laundry room. I suspect he likes the way the vibrations from the washing machines pass through the floor and up into his body. He's stroking the stubbled head of a rabbit. A tuft of stuffing protrudes from what had once been an ear. The rabbit, a discarded doll, is not long for this world.

Rupert also isn't much to look at, despite his superficial handsomeness. We don't have a high-tech assembly line, just a couple of 3D printers that have seen better days and some young people eager to try out their skills. So Rupert's gait is a little off and he has a kind of Parkinsonian twitch, not to mention all the dings and scratches he's sustained on his trips outside the community. I feel bad for him. He's only three years old, yet he walks and talks more like an octogenarian than I do.

Like all AI, he also has a couple of mysterious bugs, random ghosts in the machine. For instance, he loves stuffed animals and now carries this rabbit with him everywhere. We've tried to prevent him from taking it along when he leaves Arcadia, but he insists. So, to ensure that both his hands are free, we made him a monkey backpack whose arms wrap around his neck. For all his faults, Rupert remains extraordinarily useful, particularly on those rare external missions, and I've grown quite attached to him.

Rupert looks up as I walk in.

"Good afternoon, Rachel," he says in his posh English accent. That was Lizzie's doing—she was binge-watching episodes of the old TV show *Downton Abbey* while coding his personality. He looks like a young aristocrat down from Oxford for the weekend. "How are you today?"

"I'm a little tired," I confess. "What do you think of the recent attack, Rupert?"

He looks at me, and it's almost as if I can see his inner gears moving as he reviews and synthesizes all the available information. It takes only a few moments. "Rather a cock-up it seems. We responded quickly and effectively. And we have a Capture. You are here because you'd like me to visit her, yes? Lizzie connected me to the video feed. Her name is Karyn. She seems a proper young woman with a fondness for graphic novels."

"Could she still be a threat to the community?"

"I'd like to meet her first before I come to any definitive conclusion."

"Well, you know where she is," I say, preparing to leave. "Oh, Rupert, one more thing: how did they get through the outer perimeter?"

"I don't know."

I'm grateful that he doesn't have Karyn's bug. Rupert is fragile enough at this point that he could easily smack his head right off his neck. "It was too sophisticated for you?"

"Oh, no, Rachel. That part of the archive is not available."

I stare at him. "Not available?"

"Except for the visuals, those 10.5 seconds are not available. I'm sorry, Rachel."

"How is that possible?"

Rupert turns his attention back to the limp rabbit in his hands. "I wish I knew," he says.

"Could the attackers have disabled the virtual perimeter and simultaneously erased all evidence of their hack?"

"Yes, that is possible, but I do not see any evidence of that." He holds up the rabbit. "Do you think we can fix this, Rachel? I'm afraid that it might have been my fault."

"I'll sew it up for you tonight."

Rupert smiles. He looks quite human at that moment. He hands me the rabbit. "Shall I fetch a blowtorch and a sketchbook?"

"Yes, Rupert. Please put her through her paces. A full diagnostic."

I'd escort him back to quarantine, since I'm eager to

see his initial interaction with Karyn, but I have a more important task.

Zoltan is in the Hub, a large room off the Assembly Hall where he spends most of his time. The Hub is the nerve center of Arcadia—the above-ground one, at least. The co-chairs occupy facing tables in the center of the room, but Zoltan prefers to sit in the corner before a wall of screens. He usually has three dozen windows open conveying information from every part of Arcadia, along with international climate information, news of terrorism attacks, coding updates, and streams in several languages, as well as at least two ongoing chess games with distant partners. I suffer vertigo every time I watch him work.

Zoltan swivels around at the sound of my approach. He has a spidery physique, all arms and spindly legs. He spends so much time in front of screens that, unlike everyone else his age in Arcadia, he wears glasses. The small wire-rims make him seem even younger than he is. When he was a child, I tried to persuade him to spend some time in the sun, to no avail. Both he and Lizzie used their superlative coding skills to get out of Arcadia's manual-work requirements.

"What do you think of Karyn?" he asks.

"A conduit," I say, "for information."

"Precisely."

"And you saw how much information was generated by this attack."

"An impressive amount."

I want to surprise Zoltan with something that he doesn't know. "You realize that the kind of sublime polymer in those drones is currently in the design phase."

"I do."

"There are only a handful of outfits that could move it to the kind of operational stage we saw today."

"Actually," Zoltan smiles impishly, "there's only one."

"You knew immediately that it was CRISPR International."

"I suspected."

"It was confirmed by the breach of the perimeter," I point out. "That was no amateur hack."

"It wasn't a hack at all," Zoltan says.

I stare at him. "What do you mean?"

Zoltan looks as pleased as a new parent. He pushes his glasses up his nose. "I did that. I opened the gate and let them in."

My heart freezes.

Chapter Four

I've been an ice woman my entire life.

When the other kids in my high school stared out the window in class thinking about the beach, I dreamed of stealing back in time to stow away on the legendary expeditions of the Victorian era. I had an insatiable appetite for narratives of great suffering and achievement: the race to the South Pole, the ice-bound saga of Ernest Shackleton, Robert Peary's dogsled search for the geographic North Pole. To reproduce those experiences as best I could, I'd go on long winter hikes in the White Mountains with a small cache of dried fruit and beef jerky as well as a journal to keep an obsessive log of my daily slog. My parents and my few friends considered me a lunatic.

I was born in the wrong era. When I came of age, there were no polar adventures left. Still, as I learned during my very first year of college, I could explore downward. By taking ice core samples, I could see what Shackleton or Peary couldn't: the history that lay beneath their feet. In search of that history, I would spend as much time as I could in the frostlands.

It used to be a staple of science fiction tales that a receding polar cap would unleash some antediluvian monster that had been in the deep freeze for millions of years, or a virus with the potential to sweep the planet. The real threat turned out to be more mundane. Submerged beneath the permafrost and trapped beneath the sea ice enclosing the continental shelves in the far north are immense pools of methane. If all that ice melts, the methane will shoot up into the atmosphere in immense plumes of lethal exhalation. My initial calculations suggested that fifty gigatons of released methane would push the earth's temperature up by a degree or more. Since then the ice has indeed melted, and methane has intermittently plumed into the air. For reasons too complicated to explain, however, most of the methane remains trapped. The world has been given a temporary reprieve. My latest calculations suggest that there's at most a year left in this suspended sentence, perhaps only a few months. I've checked with a colleague in a distant institute with more resources, and he concurs.

This is my last mission: to prevent the Great Methane Cloud from forming. With the help of Zoltan, I've been running computer simulations on methods of restoring the ice cover. If CRISPR, with its Lazarus Project, can bring back the passenger pigeon, surely we can bring back the polar ice cap. I believe I've come up with an elegant solution for how to do so, though I need to stress-test the results in my lab a few more times to make sure.

Zoltan is the only person in Arcadia who knows about this research. We agreed to keep it quiet. Were it to leak out, our community could become a target. Powerful interests are invested in the current status quo. The shrinking of the ice has opened the Arctic to industries desperate to vacuum up the world's last fossil fuels and minerals. The Northwest Passage has become a lucrative shipping route. Various militaries and paramilitaries have been fighting for decades over the territory in the previously frozen north. Locking it up under ice again would effectively rebury our remaining carbon resources—an eminently wise decision that no powerful official could ever endorse.

It might seem ridiculous to maintain a status quo that will soon tip into ecocide. Greed, however, is a powerful motivator. Just ask the man with clogged arteries who orders a second helping of ice cream even though he's already short of breath and feels that telltale tightness in his chest. The treasure up north beckons like an immense hot-fudge sundae, and humanity has a deadly sweet tooth.

A number of actors, if they knew of my research, would go to great lengths to disrupt it. But the one with the most skin in the game—and the most resources to devote to maintaining the current rules of the game—is CRISPR International. This corporation, which made its mark and its money by genetically engineering away multiple sclerosis and diabetes, has grown into a conglomerate with interests everywhere. The international community has withered away, and CRISPR International seems to have taken its place.

Now it seems that CRISPR is behind the latest attack on Arcadia. That may be surprising, but not half as much as Zoltan's actions.

"I wanted to test their capabilities," he explains to me after I express my shock at his confession. "And we gathered great intel."

"So did they!" I practically scream at him.

"Yes," he says patiently, as if talking to a child. "They learned how impregnable our defenses are."

"That's what we think," I say, "out of our own arrogance."

"Their arrogance is far greater," he assures me. "Now we have one of their drones, one of their AIs, and a window into their digital capabilities. Not bad for ten minutes' work."

"Why are you telling me this? You knew I'd be furious."

"I told you because you were about to figure it out on your own," he says coolly. "And now we can work together on this, just as we've done on your computer simulations."

He doesn't want my help. Zoltan wants my silence.

In the last year, Arcadia has divided into two factions. The Traditionalists want to concentrate on self-defense, which requires latest-generation 3D printers, devices that are not cheap. To acquire such technology, we'd have to forgo our plans to expand the community by 10 percent. We'd have to earmark all our surplus food and possibly cut back on caloric intake for half a year. Then a team accompanied by Rupert and his monkey knapsack would have to make the risky journey to Montreal to make the trade. The new printer would allow us to upgrade our arsenal and, as a side benefit, upgrade Rupert as well.

Zoltan, as the leader of the Disrupters, argues that Arcadia simply doesn't have the resources to defend itself against a determined and wealthy enemy, that we will always lose any arms race. Until recently, all we had to worry about were the scruffier operators. Last year, though, thanks to my ex-husband Julian, we came to the attention of CRISPR International. It had officially hired him to produce a report on the state of the world. In fact, it really wanted to use him to get to Benjamin, our son-turned-mercenary, and prevent him from distributing one of CRISPR's life-extending technologies as widely as possible.

Zoltan has presented a plan to the Community Council to work with a group of paramilitary hackers to bring down CRISPR. He believes that the best defense is a good offense and that, as the weaker party, Arcadia has to rely on asymmetrical warfare. I'm not convinced of the Traditionalist position, but I think Zoltan's plan is worse. If we prance around the flanks of CRISPR, it will put all its considerable weight into crushing us. It's frightening enough to be in the ring with a powerful bull. It's far more dangerous if you act like a picador as well and enrage it.

The two factions in Arcadia have remained deadlocked despite several all-community meetings. We've neither taken steps to acquire the 3D printer nor contacted the hackers. I've been privately happy that this deadlock has not escalated into outright conflict. The last thing Arcadia needs now is another schism.

"Did you set your plan in motion?" I ask Zoltan.

He stares straight into my eyes and says, "Absolutely not."

"Then why do you think they just attacked us?"

"Because of you, Rachel." Do I detect a mischievous twinkle in his eye? "Because of your research."

"And how could they have learned about it? Even here in Arcadia, the only person who knows is you."

He directs my attention to one of the screens behind him. "Do you know a Bjorn Amundsen?"

"The Norwegian glaciologist."

"And you've been corresponding with him."

"He's the leading expert on methane hydrates."

"Are you aware of the paper he just published on the topic?"

I glance at the screen. "It looks useful."

"He footnoted you." Zoltan swipes the screen. "There."

I examine the footnote. It merely nods in the direction of my research. I marvel that Zoltan knows the latest advances in my field of expertise. "It's a footnote, Zoltan."

"And you don't think that CRISPR International checks out footnotes?"

"It's an obscure scientific paper."

"They have the highest-powered computers scanning

every scintilla of published material every second of the day to identify threats and opportunities."

"You're saying that CRISPR International launched an attack on the basis of a single footnote."

Zoltan shrugs. "You of all people should appreciate the importance of footnotes. Anyway, that's my best guess. And it will remain my best guess until you supply me with a better one."

I do have a better guess, but I'm not going to tell Zoltan because it involves him. Instead, I reveal only part of my hand: "Here's my guess. You're going to announce that CRISPR was behind today's attack. And then you will renew your proposal to ally with hackers to bring down the most powerful corporation in the world."

Zoltan is nodding. "And you're going to support me this time."

"Because of the footnote?"

"Among other things."

I need to buy time to finish my project. My project is more important than Zoltan's crazy scheme, more important even than Arcadia.

"Okay, Zoltan, but we'll need to build a stronger case. Today has exhausted me. Let's meet tomorrow to work this out."

Zoltan looks pleased. He thinks that he has turned an otherwise weak pawn into a key player in his attack. He can afford to be magnanimous.

"Of course, Rachel. I apologize for throwing so much at

you at once. Let's meet for breakfast. Will eight AM be too early for you?"

"Let's say lunch." I stifle a yawn. "I think I might be sleeping late tomorrow morning."

Zoltan readily agrees. I note the glint of pity in his eyes, the pity that the young have for the old.

As for me, I'm not tired at all. I've plenty of energy for the two tasks ahead of me. I need to fix Rupert's stuffed animal. And I've got to take a short trip via virtual reality.

Chapter Five

Transcript of conversation between Rachel Leopold and Emmanuel Puig, director of the World Geo-Paleontology Association.

Brussels, December 15, 2051

Rachel Leopold: This is safe?

Emmanuel Puig: I have the assurance of my IT people.

Rachel: I have to be sure that this is 100 percent safe.

Emmanuel: Look in the top left corner of your security screen. I'm now signing us both up for a third-party verifier. There, you see. All clear.

Rachel: Okay. Thank you. And thank you for meeting me here in Brussels. My daughter and her children will come to this park in fifteen minutes.

Emmanuel: It's a pleasure to meet you face to face after all these years. Well, avatar to avatar. You're exactly how I imagined you.

Rachel: Really? I was in a hurry today, so I just used the default avatar for "seniors." I believe that what you're looking at right now is

Judi Dench. She was one of my favorite actresses back in the day.

Emmanuel: Oh, my apologies. I should have chosen George Clooney. But you're looking at the real Emmanuel Puig. Well, minus a few things that I've airbrushed out.

Rachel: We don't have a lot of time, so let me cut to the chase. You contacted me last year after my husband's death. I apologize for not responding. Are you still putting together his… materials?

Emmanuel: Yes. Your son Gordon generously shared the full version of your husband's final report with me. It was very helpful for my latest book, which just came out this year. I can send you a—

Rachel: It's not necessary. What are you going to do with Julian's report?

Emmanuel: I'd like to publish it one day soon. It will be an important contribution to the field he founded. I was even thinking of calling it *Splinterlands* as an homage to his original masterpiece. Of course, since I will provide annotations, I'd naturally like to ask you some questions about…

Rachel: Later. Right now, I'm interested in something else. As you know, Julian sent me a coded message along with the report. So that I wouldn't get fooled by CRISPR.

Emmanuel: It was quite clever of him.

Rachel: Well, a stopped clock is clever twice a day, I suppose.

Emmanuel: You're still angry about…

Rachel: I don't have time for regrets. What I do want to know is this: do you think he also sent coded messages to our children? Or do you think there are coded messages in his report?

Emmanuel: About?

Rachel: About CRISPR.

Emmanuel: What kind of coded messages?

Rachel: Well, for instance, do you know where he was when he sent those notes to the children and me?

Emmanuel: He spoke of the capital of the Northern Territory, so I'm assuming he was in Darwin. The former Australia.

Rachel: Do we know where in Darwin?

Emmanuel: CRISPR maintains a complex in the hills above the city.

Rachel: Is there any possibility he might have sent more detailed information in code about the location?

Emmanuel: For what reason? He was dying. He didn't think anyone would be able to find him before he... passed away.

Rachel: This is just a guess. The coded message that he sent me, the verse about the narrow gate and the wide gate, was from Matthew. From the Bible. There's another verse, just after that one, that I used to quote all the time. I even mentioned it once in congressional testimony.

Emmanuel: I am not familiar with the Bible.

Rachel: It goes like this: "Everyone who hears these words of mine and does not put them into practice is like a foolish person who builds his house on sand. The rain comes down, the streams rise. The winds blow and beat against that house, and it falls with a great crash."

Emmanuel: That sounds like the opening of his report. Your house in Washington. During Hurricane Donald.

Rachel: Exactly. That was what first caught my attention. But now I think he was referring to a different house. The house of CRISPR. It's just a guess. I think he knew that CRISPR International would continue to be a threat to his family. Perhaps he wanted to give me the tools to bring that house down with a great crash. Could you take a look at those materials of his and see if there's anything in them that looks like a code? A strange phrase. An alpha-numeric string.

Emmanuel: I'm not a cryptologist, but I'd be happy to see what our IT department can find.

Rachel: Can we meet at the same time tomorrow in Yinchuan City?

Emmanuel: You'll be visiting your son Gordon?

Rachel: I appreciate your help, Mr. Puig.

Emmanuel: Anything I can do, Ms. Leopold. In exchange, perhaps...

Rachel: Yes?

Emmanuel: A report. When you are finished. A report for me. I'm thinking of producing a series of...

Rachel: Of course. If there is time.

Chapter Six

My daughter is trying hard to look happy about my unexpected visit. Aurora has a poet's introversion wrapped in a sociologist's dyspepsia. She doesn't smile a lot.

Still, she attempts a joke on seeing my borrowed avatar. "Mother, you don't look like yourself these days!"

My grandchildren air-kiss me on both virtual cheeks with no hesitation. They haven't seen me since they were infants and everyone over the age of eighty no doubt looks the same to them. My Judi Dench avatar is as good an image of a grandmother as anyone else in this shapeshifting age. They're teenagers now, and both sport the latest fashion. Emil is a Mondrian from head to toe, a jazzy assortment of colorful boxes. Étienne is the night sky, constellations wrapping around his arms and legs. Needless to say, I don't get it: kids change their bodypaper as frequently as they change their clothes. Some even make money as living billboards. What's wrong with the skin they're born in?

They politely report on their incomprehensible lives—much of it virtual—and then take their leave to mingle with the other young people milling around us. Soon they're playing some game that, in mixing the seen and the unseen, has them leaping and cavorting like mad mimes. I can't help but see it all as a tremendous waste of energy.

Aurora and I are sitting on a park bench in South Brussels, where my daughter has lived much of her adult life. The park is in the middle of the Zone Verte, the only truly safe sector of the city.

It's not my first time using VR. I took several return trips to Antarctica to look at conditions on the ground. (Once I would have said, "conditions on the ice," but that's no longer accurate.) This is, however, my first time VRing to an urban setting and actually interacting with other people. I feel like an apparition—in a city packed with ghosts.

It was bad enough when I visited Brussels in person after the births of Étienne and then Emil, extravagantly expensive flights that Arcadia gave me as a thank-you for my service. I'd become completely unaccustomed to the rhythms of a city: the frenetic rush to jobs, to meetings, to shops, everyone as urgently focused as if they were fleeing a disaster. I vaguely remembered doing this myself years before, when I lived in Washington, DC—until I realized I was only running in place.

The most baffling feature of that short trip to Brussels was the multiplicity of screens. Every square foot of public space was dominated by moving images—music videos, deodorant advertisements, trailers for the next *Star Wars* installment. Most appalling were the offers to VR to current at-risk areas of the world to watch them disappear beneath the waves. I'd grown used to the pace of life in Arcadia by then, where we were largely unplugged from the relentless effort to "capture eyeballs." In Brussels, I felt as if my eyeballs were swatted around like squash balls before being returned, the worse for wear, to their sockets.

Now, on this VR excursion, I can see that everything has been raised by a power of ten. As if the city weren't crowded enough, avatars glide around, gawking, in an endless stream. I wish I knew how to turn on the unsee function. I'm assaulted not only by the sight of all these virtual tourists but by the virtual ads that target them. "Come to the Zone Rouge!" screams one as it unfurls just above the playground sandbox. "See live death!" The scene that unscrolls beneath the headline is so disturbing I have to look away. I try to focus on Aurora, but I'm distracted by a talking orangutan that interrupts our conversation with a pitch for the latest chemo pills. Aurora finally offers me instructions on how to turn off the ads so we can talk in peace.

After the orangutan disappears, I ask, "Everyone is healthy and safe?"

"You can see how happy Emil and Étienne are, and Maxime is doing fine." Though she's still trying to smile, I can see that Aurora is anxious about something specific. "So, to what do we owe this unexpected pleasure?"

Ah, she must think I'm going to give her some bad news. Why else would I show up with less than a day's notice?

I hasten to reassure her. "I'm fine, and Arcadia's fine. Really, you ought to think of joining me there."

Relieved, Aurora rolls her eyes. It's not the first time I've tried to persuade her to move the family to Vermont. My daughter hates slipping into old arguments.

"We're about to expand," I tell her. "The new annex will house another twenty-five people. As an Original Member, I can get all four of you on the waiting list. But I'll need to know now."

"Really, mother, and what would I do in Arcadia? I'm sure that you have a great demand for sociologists."

"You could continue your research. As long as..."

"As long as I do something *productive*. Like weed the garden. I can't do that, mother. I'm hopeless. Put me down on a desert island and I'd be dead in a day. Same with Maxime."

Her husband is a medievalist with a fondness for parkour and kinetic neuropop. It's hard to imagine him fitting into our quiet community. Still, I persist.

"It's something you could learn. The children, too, of course. Think of them. What do you imagine Brussels will look like in ten years? The Zone Verte will have shrunk to a couple of blocks. All that frenzy, all that loneliness packed into a space the size of a football stadium."

Aurora's patience evaporates. "I'm not interested in going back to nature, mother. Yes, from your perspective, this is an anarchic society, but we've learned how to live here."

"Live?" I look around. "With screens everywhere? With talking orangutans?"

"You're too focused on the surfaces. It's what takes place hidden from view that matters."

"The poverty? The violence?"

"The scrubbers that clean our apartment. The fully automated factories that produce everything we need in the dark, twenty-four hours a day. This is modern life. I refuse to go backward. I refuse to join you in the fourteenth century. Here, we are free to think."

"Arcadia is hardly the Dark Ages," I say, summoning up images of our weaponry, our computerized defenses, our imperfect Rupert. "We keep up with the times, but we also eat real apples, not the seaweed simulacra you're stuck with. And we can think for ourselves, thank you very much."

Aurora sighs with exasperation, as though she'd failed once again to describe a rainbow to a blind person. "At this point, we're used to mock chicken and fake broccoli. It's all sufficiently nutritious. And when real apples are beyond reach, fruit leather seems just as good as the original. Honestly, I think the kids would prefer the simulacrum."

"We have an orchard that produces twelve different kinds of apples," I tell her, and then proceed to sing the praises of each variety. "Imagine introducing Emil to the Honeycrisp and Étienne to the Fuji..."

I didn't, of course, come all the way to Brussels to talk

about apples. Nor am I interested in repeating the arguments my daughter and I have had so many times before. What I'm doing, though Aurora doesn't know it, is establishing my cover story just in case anyone is watching. I have to assume that someone's always watching.

That's why, while I'm talking apples, I DM my daughter.

I've never direct messaged anyone before, nor have I ever been so concerned about security that I needed to send a text directly to someone's retinal implant. But now I'm worried—and not only about the capabilities of CRISPR International. I'm also concerned that the corporation has someone working inside Arcadia. Rupert showed me how to set up the message on a burner account before I left so that I could send it, encrypted, with a flick of my ghostly finger at any point during my VR trip. He assures me that DMs remain the most secure method of communication in this age of perpetual surveillance.

Fortunately, my daughter is thoroughly modern, and that includes the de rigueur retinal implant that allows her to browse the Web, receive DMs, and even access many VR features with a blink of her eye. For once I'm grateful for that.

While I ramble on about my favorite apple varieties, I watch my daughter's expression. She's squinting slightly as she reads the message, scrolling down her retinal display as if she were reading an email or a news feed. The message is short, so it doesn't take her long to finish it. Before I can make it through the entire litany of Arcadian apples, her gaze has refocused on me.

"Oh, well, you certainly don't need to hear any more about apples, do you?" I say.

She's thinking. I can see that she's having difficulty processing the new information while continuing to chat. She needs help.

"Let's see what my grandchildren are doing," I suggest. "I miss them so very much."

With relief, Aurora leads my avatar to the center of the park, where Emil and Étienne are engaged in their elaborate dance. At least it looks like a dance to me. They are throwing invisible objects to one another, sometimes catching them, sometimes avoiding them, sometimes using them to build something equally invisible. They're operating on a VR level I don't have access to. In Arcadia, young people have continued playing real volleyball and basketball. I don't even understand the appeal of these virtual games. We stand and watch, and I wish I could take Aurora's hand in mine. It's been so long since we touched.

Our apple orchards are dying. That's something I haven't bothered to tell Aurora. All our delicious varieties will soon be gone if the temperatures continue to rise. The McIntosh trees, which need nearly a thousand hours of temperatures below forty-five degrees in order to bud in the spring, have already stopped producing. The Dorsett Golden and Tropic Sweet, which need only three hundred hours, continue to generate reasonable yields—but I just don't know for how long. Vermont has gone from apples

to citrus in a single generation. In the long run, barring
something unexpected, Arcadia will prove as unsustainable
as Brussels. Of course, as the economists used to say, in the
long run we're all dead.

My husband Julian West, a fan of that dismal science,
chronicled in detail the fragmenting of the world. He was
the worst kind of academic: all talk, no action. Remember Nero and his fiddle? Julian tapped, tapped, tapped at
his laptop while the world burned. During our marriage
he barely acknowledged climate change, and when he finally did, it was too late. He treated my research into ice
with bemusement, much as my fellow Arcadians treat it
today. For him, history only happened north of the equator,
among people who read Tolstoy, Gibbon, and Fukuyama.
I tried to tell him about the likely impact of climate refugees on the hitherto stable societies of Europe, the United
States, and Northeast Asia. I showed him forecast maps
of resource wars over water, arable land, and rare earth
minerals. They had only a modest impact on his seminal
work, *Splinterlands*. Only in his final report, sent on what
was to be his last day on earth, did I notice that he took
climate—and the natural world more generally—with true
seriousness. At one point he even compared the fracturing
of the international community to the calving of a glacier.
What a bittersweet reference. If he'd only shown that kind
of appreciation of my world thirty years earlier, perhaps our
marriage might have had a chance.

I don't think Aurora takes climate change seriously,

either. Oh, she believes in it—skepticism is no longer an option—but she's told me that Brussels is safe since it's sufficiently far from the coast and remains part of a still-temperate band of habitation. It hasn't entirely slipped into the zone of poverty and conflict that has spread like the desert sands across much of the red-hot waistline of the world. Yes, the city managed to survive last year's PNC3 staph epidemic with almost no casualties, thanks to a strict quarantine. But Aurora is wrong to think that Brussels is invulnerable.

I've watched the Zone Verte recede over the years like Lake Baikal or the Dead Sea, their life-giving waters drying up and the mud taking over. In the Zone Rouge, football thugs and refugee clans battle for control of decaying neighborhoods that city services no longer reach. Gentrification occasionally reclaims a previously dangerous set of blocks, forcing the poets and the poor to move further out, but that's the exception. The Zone Verte gets ever smaller and more crowded. Meanwhile, the newest residential skyscrapers tower over the remaining baroque palaces and Art Deco buildings that attract a diminishing flow of Asian tourists. Most of the city's revenues derive from financial services and the tax levied on virtual visitors like me, who slip in for a few hours to visit family or get a shot of carefully curated Old World charm. Brussels has become the European equivalent of the Native American reservations of America's past, with their casinos and dusty tourist attractions.

I'd rather see Aurora and her family move somewhere safe, like Xinjiang, where her brother Gordon lives. If I had any money, I'd set them up in a Himalayan mountain village or a new resort in the Kalahari. Actually, I think Gordon has already attempted to do something like that, but Aurora is stubborn. She clings to her dream of European cosmopolitanism. Her children are fluent in French, English, and Dutch. She updates me on her dalliances with the city's literary avant-garde. I feel as though I'm getting letters from a Jewish family in fin-de-siècle Vienna. It's a vanishing world. If the Zone Verte doesn't turn Rouge altogether, then the political extremists will take over Wallonia and forcibly eject Aurora and her family. The status quo of Brussels, like that of the planet as a whole, is as fragile as a dripping icicle.

"They've grown up so fast," I murmur to Aurora. "You should at least bring them on a virtual visit to Arcadia."

Aurora turns toward me. "I miss Daddy."

This is her way of signaling me. Perhaps she does miss Julian, though I doubt she would ever express it this way. They did not have a particularly good relationship. She always blamed him for pushing her into academia instead of supporting her desire to become a poet. Better that than to blame herself for a failure of nerve.

"I miss him, too," I say.

I don't actually miss the last version of my husband, the one I saw shortly before his death. But I do miss the Julian West I met when I was a graduate student, the one with whom I talked late into the night about how we would conquer the intellectual universe, just the two of us, social history and hard science standing back to back in a barroom brawl against the ignorant of the world.

I miss that earlier version of myself, as well. I miss the world as it was.

"Do you remember all the funny little things he used to say?" Aurora asks.

"We should have written them down," I say, preparing myself for the message.

"There was one that came back to me just this morning. Of every four opportunities, only one will pan out. Even if that one is the least promising, you should seize the opportunity with all your might."

"I remember that one," I say. "What made you think of it?"

"I don't know." Aurora crosses her arms and shivers. "I really can't remember."

We're interrupted again, this time not by an orangutan but by the two adolescents. Emil now looks like an ancient Soviet propaganda poster, all red and Cyrillic, while Étienne is covered with hieroglyphics like an Egyptian tomb painting. Their game is over, and they are excited to tell us how well they did.

I understand nothing, but I'm happy to listen. I'm happy to have this brief illusion of family life.

Chapter Seven

"Here," I say to Rupert. "The operation was successful."

Rupert receives the repaired rabbit with all the gravity of a scientist accepting a Nobel Prize. "Thank you," he says as he submits the rabbit to a critical examination. "It is beautiful."

Rupert lacks the fine motor skills to fix a stuffed animal. If we had the latest 3D printer, we could upgrade his hands, perhaps even eliminate his Parkinsonian twitches with a new operating system. He probably has only another year or two before his mobility becomes seriously compromised. It's easy to forget that Rupert is not human, given his good looks, plummy Oxbridge accent, and endearing bugs. The most human thing about him, however, is his mortality.

"How was your visit with Karyn?"

"We had a most pleasant tête-à-tête, Rachel. But she is quite odd."

"How so?"

"There is so much she doesn't know. And she can be quite violent with herself when she can't answer a question."

"Who do you think made her?"

"She was made by a design firm called InfoMatrix. They contract with many corporations."

"Date of manufacture?"

"November 15, 2051. She was turned on at 8:51 a.m."

"So she's just a newborn. Do you know who bought her?"

"I do not."

"Does she have any special features?"

"Her eyes can receive and process information in all known spectra. Her ears are extremely sensitive, too, and can pick up subatomic vibrations. Her nose can detect parts per trillion. These are impressive specifications." Rupert's head trembles, as if he's overcome with envy.

"Is she unique in these respects?"

"Sensory capabilities at that level of complexity are not available for sale or download."

"Can she hurt our community?"

"No. Like me, she is programmed with the 'do no harm' directive."

After the wave of killer bots of the late 2020s, all AI have this feature. Still, some rogue bots do remain in circulation, and a few nonstate actors refuse to adhere to the protocol. Programmed with older code no longer in the public domain, these killer bots don't look much like humans. Most often they're just microdrones with DNA targeting, capable of delivering toxins as quietly as mosquitos. Arcadia's outer perimeter, after many upgrades over the years, can distinguish between such drones and the real insects that it allows into the community.

"Is there any way she can send information out?"

"Those capabilities have been disabled," Rupert assures me.

"Why was she given human form? They could have made a sphere or even a drone with the same capabilities."

"I don't know."

"Can she weld?"

"Rather poorly. Arcadia has better welders."

"Should we turn her into scrap metal?"

Rupert seems to consider this question. He looks down at his rabbit. He looks up at me. "If she is disassembled, some of her parts could enhance my capabilities."

"Would you like that?"

"There are pluses and minuses to such a plan."

"Or she could be your companion."

"Yes," Rupert says. "Yes, I think that I would prefer that alternative."

"Then that will be my recommendation," I tell him.

Rupert says nothing. He strokes the nubby gray surface of the rabbit. I wish I could say that I was just being compassionate. But I've begun to formulate a plan that involves our new Spongebot.

It's midmorning in Arcadia. I had to get up early to use the VR equipment to go to Brussels. I'm meeting Zoltan for lunch, so I have a little time to figure out what my daughter was trying to tell me.

She'd said, "Out of every four opportunities, only one will pan out. And even if that one is the least promising of the four, you should seize that opportunity with all your might."

My husband, Julian, never said anything of the sort. In my DM, I'd asked Aurora if he'd sent her any unusual messages that she couldn't decipher. While we were watching Emil and Étienne in the park, she must have been reviewing his final message and any other communications she'd received from him.

Now it's up to me to figure out what her enigmatic statement means. And as yet, I haven't a clue. I go back to the chapter of Matthew. Nothing leaps out at me about ones or fours. I ask Rupert, giving him access to all my correspondence with Julian, *Splinterlands,* and Julian's final report for CRISPR. Rupert has nothing to offer.

"Don't give up," he tells me. "That is what your former husband seems to be saying."

There's only one person in Arcadia who might have a shot at deciphering Julian's code—if indeed it is a code. But he's the only one person I can't share this information with.

Zoltan is waiting for me in the foyer of the cafeteria. Lunch is leftover venison stew, plus the season's remaining fresh apples baked into a crumble. I think of the seaweed substitutes that Aurora and her family put up with. We Arcadians seldom appreciate just how good we have it. More than one person last night complained that the venison was too chewy.

"You were up early today," Zoltan says as we bring our trays to one of the rooms on the second-floor balcony of the cafeteria, where we can have some privacy.

"Early to bed, early to rise," I say.

"Did you enjoy your little trip?"

It's the unexpected opening gambit that I'd already anticipated. I know he always checks the VR logs. "I've been meaning to see my grandchildren for some time. The attack yesterday reminded me that I'm not immortal."

Zoltan is eyeing me. He suspects something. But then, so do I. Now it's my turn to make a surprise move.

"Speaking of family, have you been in touch with yours?"

Zoltan clears his throat. "My mother is fine," he says tentatively. "She prefers her smaller community."

I'm sure she does. Since they left nearly a decade ago, the Horvaths have been a subject largely avoided in Arcadia. They were Original Members who decamped with a dozen other OMs and their families in 2042. At the time I feared our community would fall victim to the same forces tearing apart societies all over the world, but we survived. We continue to have our divisions, but they're containable, like the tomato blight.

"How *is* the Farm?"

"Surviving. They keep asking me to join them there."

"But you don't."

"Arcadia's my family now."

All those years ago, I was convinced that Zoltan had remained behind because he preferred to master the technology we have here. It wasn't clear then what kind of new community the Horvaths and the other schismatics wanted to create, although they were clearly technology-averse. Now I'm not so sure of Zoltan's motivation in staying. But I know I've gotten all the information he's going to offer, so I move on.

"What have you learned from the data you collected during the breach?" I ask.

"They're going to attack again."

"When?"

"Sooner rather than later. They believe you're close to a solution."

"How could they possibly know that?"

"From Bjorn Amundsen."

"Bjorn would never cooperate with CRISPR."

Zoltan pushes his device across the table. I'm looking at a frantic message from Hilda Amundsen saying that her husband has gone missing. Zoltan indicates the initial post in the chain. "I was trying to get in touch with Amundsen and instead I received this message from his wife. It's what CRISPR does when it needs information. Whisks people off for some quality face time."

"Bjorn knows next to nothing about my research."

"The timing of his disappearance correlates with yesterday's attack."

"You didn't need to open up the outer perimeter to get that information."

"True," Zoltan concedes, "but we also learned this."

He makes a few swipes on his device, and now I'm looking at a lot of coding that I can't understand.

"And this is?"

"It's a list of all the electronic signatures of our computer defenses. It's part of the massive data packet that the drones and our new friend Karyn sent before we shut them down."

I can barely contain my anger. "The keys to the kingdom, in other words."

"Don't worry, I changed the locks," Zoltan says.

"But now that they know the parameters, they can deploy high-powered code breakers."

"Theoretically, but that would take time."

"I still fail to see the value of inviting them into the castle bailey."

"Appear weak when you are strong," Zoltan says. "That's Sun Tzu."

"Don't be a horse's ass," I counter. "That's my grandmother Ida."

"I dare say I'm a better chess player than either you or your grandmother."

"Is that how you win at chess? By deliberately sacrificing your pawns and exposing your king?"

"If necessary. If I'm playing someone who knows all the traditional openings and is always one step ahead of me. In such cases, you can only win with the unexpected move."

It's time for me to be bold, too. "Let me provide you with a different interpretation of what you've told me so far." Zoltan looks annoyed but remains silent. "I think Bjorn was confirming something that CRISPR already suspected. And they suspected something because someone here tipped them off."

"Interesting." Zoltan leans back from the table and folds his arms. "Because that's what I think, too."

"But the only people who know about the project are you and me."

We stare at each other. I suspect him. And he suspects—what?

Zoltan says, "I think we have a sleeper."

"And what evidence do you have of that?"

He pulls his device back to his side of the table and swipes a few more times. "I haven't yet shown this to anyone. It's a list of direct messages sent from Arcadia over the last two years."

He turns the device around so that I can see the list of encrypted DMs from the approximate geolocation of our community. My name is on the bottom of the list.

I expected him to inspect the VR logs, but I didn't think he had access to the DMs. So much for the security of Rupert's burner account. "I contacted my daughter," I tell Zoltan, striving to keep my voice calm. "To let her know that I was coming."

"You're missing the point," he says, his finger dancing over what I now see is the same name highlighted over and over again in yellow.

Bertrand.

I shake my head. Not Bertrand. He's the last person who would turn against the community that welcomed him in. "Betray his own daughter?"

"What better way to win our trust than to contribute flesh and blood to the community?"

"This doesn't prove anything. You don't know where the DMs went, or their content."

"I'm working on that," Zoltan says. "I think I can get geolocations for some of the addressees. But even without that information, I can ask the question: Who is Bertrand DMing and why has his DM activity gone up in the last month?"

"You think he's been a sleeper for twenty years? And this is the first time he's done anything suspicious?"

"That's what sleepers do. They sleep. Until they're awoken."

"Have you confronted him?"

"Not yet. I want to gather more information first. And I don't want to distract from the urgent task before us."

"Preparing for CRISPR's next attack."

"Oh no, the best defense is a—"

"Of course, you want to attack first." I should have anticipated that move. "With the Movement's help."

"But first I need your help at the Council meeting to-day. I want to provide the Movement with all the digital information we gathered from CRISPR's attack. It should be enough to bring down CRISPR's network worldwide."

"Even though the Movement is part of the problem, not part of the solution."

"Right now CRISPR is the main threat to us."

"And you think I'll support you because?"

"Because if they know that your research project pre-cipitated CRISPR's attack, the Council will put a lock on your lab. At least that's the solution I would support, as co-chair."

"I'll simply explain the importance of the research."

Zoltan smiles. "They're panicking, Rachel. They won't even be able to understand what you're talking about or why it's important. It's quite simple: If you want to save the world, you're going to have to save Arcadia first. And if you want to save Arcadia, you'll need to back my plan."

Check.

Chapter Eight

I have to admit: I don't know what Zoltan's game is.

He's been the only one in the community to help me with my research project. But has he been doing so only to provide CRISPR with continuous updates on my progress? He's also been an advocate for siding with the Movement to take down CRISPR, but for all I know he could be working with CRISPR to take down the Movement. Or—and this is an even darker thought—has he been conspiring with his family to take over Arcadia? Maybe Zoltan's been the sleeper all along.

I've never been very good at chess. I can see only one or two moves ahead before I'm undone by the branching possibilities. I may well be a pawn in Zoltan's larger game, but to protect my research project, I'm the one who has to make a sacrifice. At the emergency Council meeting this evening, I speak in favor of his plan.

Anuradha is plainly shocked by my reversal. After the

vote, which goes narrowly in Zoltan's favor, she's more abrupt than usual when she invites me on our weekly evening constitutional.

It's a balmy December night, the temperature in the upper fifties, the new normal for northern Vermont. She's wearing a mauve sari and has a wrap around her shoulders against the evening chill. Her dress must have been exotic indeed when she first moved to this part of Vermont, where dairy farmers, male and female, favor jeans and flannel shirts. Her saris, however, anticipated the hotter summers and milder winters of the new Northeast. She makes them herself, with silk harvested from the silkworm farm she established long ago in an unused milking shed attached to the silo. The dyes come from the fruits we grow, the mauve from the mulberries whose leaves feed the silkworms.

It's but one of the many ways Anuradha has led by doing. Arcadia was her idea, although she's always insisted it was a collective effort from the start. For all her commitment to collective action, however, she refuses to let the natural inertia of the group prevent progress. She never says "someone should," only "I will." If not for Anuradha, I might have long ago given up on this community and its myriad internecine struggles. If she could endure the compromises of group living for the greater good, then so could I.

I shrink from disappointing her, and tonight she's disappointed. I can tell from the fussy way she wraps her shawl around her shoulders and the pinched tone she uses to address me.

We're taking our usual path around the duck pond/fishery. It's dark, our way lit only by the full moon and the few solar lights that run along the side closer to the water. She takes my arm and we walk slowly. The path is smooth. I know it well, so I'm not afraid of falling.

"You switched sides, Rachel. Why?"

I've already prepared my cover story. "I was afraid after yesterday's attack. That changed the calculus."

"If CRISPR wants to destroy us, they will, but we shouldn't give them a reason to do so."

"I'm beginning to think that it's us or them at this point."

"That's precisely the kind of bipolar thinking we've tried so hard to avoid here." Anuradha's fingers tighten around my bicep as if to reinforce her point. "Zoltan has his virtues, I don't deny it, and we're fortunate that the next generation is so capable, particularly when it comes to modern technology. But I fear that he believes that all the world's a chessboard. A black-and-white world."

"You know I agree with you," I say.

Then I take a breath and hold it. I very much want to tell Anuradha about my research. We talk about everything else on these walks: our families, our frailties, our fears, everything but that. It's not that she wouldn't understand the details. A biologist by training, she certainly would grasp the basic science behind my technique. But I've known from the start how potentially dangerous my research is. If I hadn't needed sophisticated number-crunching, I wouldn't have told anyone. I reached out to Rupert's predecessor for help with the math, but he didn't have the necessary programming skills. Lizzie was still too young when I needed that initial assistance. So that left Zoltan. As it was, I didn't explain why the quantitative analysis was so important for me. Yet, though he was only nineteen at the time, he figured it out by himself.

I exhale and continue. "But I think we should see how far we get with Zoltan's gambit."

I can't see Anuradha's face in the darkness, but I suspect her expression is one of sorrow.

We walk on in silence for a few minutes. I listen to a fish breaking the surface of the pond, a duck shaking water from its feathers. I miss the chorus of frogs.

"We can't just think of our generation," Anuradha begins. "Or the generation of Zoltan and Lizzie. We must think of the seventh generation. We must always ask ourselves: Is what I am doing good for the seventh generation?"

It's a favorite topic of Anuradha's. I murmur agreement.

"Arcadia is built for the seventh generation. We are not only carbon-neutral, we're reforesting this whole quadrant. If you add in our carbon-dioxide removal units, we're undoing the damage done over the last hundred years in this part of the country."

"Yes, and it still isn't enough. Not by a long shot."

"If we're talking about the next hundred years, of course

not. But if we're talking about the seventh generation."

"It still isn't enough."

"Let's say we add fifty more people every twenty years. Then let's say that we inspire other communities. We begin with an arithmetic progress. Then at some point, it becomes geometric. We start small and go from there."

"We don't have enough time to wait for the arithmetic to turn geometric."

Anuradha sounds impatient even as she counsels patience. "It's not a quick fix. As you've said yourself, there are no green swans."

I have indeed said that many times. For the last seventy-five years, the world has awaited its green swan—the unexpected discovery that will radically alter the climate-change equation. First it was solar power, but that didn't stop the use of fossil fuels. Then it was carbon-dioxide-removal facilities that would turn greenhouse gasses into pellets of calcium carbonate, but the technology couldn't be scaled up sufficiently. And, always, there has been the false hope of geoengineering, of tweaking nature itself so that it can solve the problem we created for ourselves. Unfortunately, these all proved to be false dreams of mastery.

As Anuradha continues to lecture me on the theme of the seventh generation, I suddenly understand the real reason I've never told her about my research project. She would be furious at me. What have I been doing but a sophisticated version of geoengineering? Haven't I succumbed to quick fix–ism myself? It hardly matters that I believe my plan will work—that a hitherto unappreciated feature of ice-crystal formation, if nudged in the right direction, might reverse the ice-albedo effect, restoring the polar ice caps and preventing all that trapped methane from pushing the earth past the point of no return. After all, what use is it to talk of the seventh generation if we're on the verge of a sixth great extinction?

This afternoon, between my lunch with Zoltan and the emergency Council meeting, I'd squeezed in just enough lab time to apply the results of Zoltan's last round of calculations. I had stimulated ice-crystal formation in above-freezing conditions and verified those results numerous times. Now I can control the spread of this crystalline frost precisely, along all three spatial axes. We ran the numbers on how large the polar caps would need to be to recreate a homeostatic ice-albedo effect, reduce global temperatures to what they had been a hundred years ago, and then stabilize them at that level. In other words, I just verified to my satisfaction that we might actually be able to bring the planet back from the edge of the furnace without plunging it into a deep freeze. I've always told myself that I was just experimenting at the margins. But now I have to be honest: I've caught sight of a green swan. I've touched its soft feathers. It's as real as you or me.

"Do you see what I mean, Rachel?" Anuradha concludes.

"I do," I say. And I do.

But perhaps because I'm eighty years old and mistakenly equating my diminishing lifespan with the planet's, I feel that Zoltan is right too. He's worried about CRISPR. I'm worried about methane. Either way, we'll need to act fast.

"And yet you voted against our best interests. Our decisions have consequences."

"Sometimes, if presented with two bad choices, we just have to pick the lesser of two evils," I point out.

"But that's exactly the bipolar thinking we should avoid!"

Of course, she's right. By choosing the lesser of two evils—an inadequately moderate response to climate change instead of outright denial—the world signed a death warrant for many island nations, ensured that dozens of countries fell apart at the seams, and added fuel to conflagrations across the globe. We didn't stand up to evil, of the greater or lesser varieties. We didn't have the courage. I've always thought, though, that the smallest subset of *we*, the *we* of Arcadia, had done the right thing. Now Anuradha is telling me that I and many of my fellow Arcadians have succumbed to the same errors of thinking that have doomed the rest of the planet.

"I was right about the Captures, wasn't I?" I respond, desperate to end this uncomfortable conversation.

"It's apples and oranges."

"Perhaps. But let's give Zoltan's plan a little time to see if it works."

I say this even though I know how little time we probably have. I say it even though I secretly intend to find out what side Zoltan is really on, and whether his plan is a lesser or a greater evil.

Chapter Nine

The security is beyond lax. That's the first thing I notice about the Farm. No elaborate VR vetting. No Quarantine Room. No high-tech perimeters. There's only a rather old-fashioned stone wall that a determined intruder could breach with nothing more sophisticated than a ladder.

"Just trees around here," Ilona explains in heavily accented English as she gives me a tour of the greenhouses. "The logging here ended twenty years ago, and even then this part of the Piscataquis County was very much uninhabited. I do not think there were even 200 people living in an area almost twice the size of your Vermont. So forget about anyone just bumping up into us."

The Farm is indeed located in a remote corner of a Maine forest. It's too far away from Arcadia for any physical connection, and I'm not sure we would have maintained one even if this renegade offshoot were just down the road. Its founders, including Ilona and her husband, Aladar, left

Arcadia almost a decade ago, along with thirty other dissenters. The split was painful. Even now I detect frostiness in Ilona's attitude toward me. She was hesitant when I first contacted her about the visit. I emphasized the urgency of the situation, though, and she relented. I suspect she did so only to get an independent update on her son Zoltan.

Ilona and Aladar were mathematicians recently arrived from Hungary when they joined Arcadia. They'd been environmentalists in their home country, part of an international scientific project to model the effects of climate change. They'd decided to leave Hungary because of the increasing discrimination that Aladar, a Roma, was facing. They thought the United States would be safe. After only a couple years at Dartmouth, however, growing anti-immigration sentiment and know-nothingism sent them into double exile—to Arcadia. And then into triple exile on the Farm.

Like me, Ilona is in charge of the greenhouses. We trade stories about tomato blight, about yields and seed saving. It helps to have at least one common interest when you're straining to be civil. The Farm is much smaller than Arcadia, only sixty people, but it maintains nearly as many greenhouses. In the decade it's been in operation, they've managed to clear only modest acreage for planting. Cutting down trees and pulling out stumps is a laborious process, Ilona explains. And the Farm doesn't have the luxury of nearby communities to trade with. Since it's even more self-contained than Arcadia, greenhouse production is that much more essential to the community's survival.

The Farm can ill afford to let its members spend their time on frivolities like coding AI. Ilona admits that they still do maintain a few screens for communication purposes. Courtesy of technology Arcadia once provided, part of the community is also VR-enabled, from the conference room in the Common House along a path to the greenhouses. This is fortunate, since I don't have time to apply to use one of Arcadia's two functioning hovercars to make the round trip. The technology has also proved fortunate for the Farm: In the community's second year, Ilona had to deal with an unfamiliar root rot that threatened their first crop. Catastrophe was averted thanks to a VR visit from an old friend in Budapest, who immediately diagnosed the problem.

Aside from these concessions to the modern age, the Farm could belong to another century altogether. The structures I can see from the path to the greenhouse are rough-hewn: no solar paint, only a few old crystalline silicon panels, and smoke rising in tendrils out of chimneys. Rudimentary construction equipment—shovels, a wheelbarrow—lies scattered in the mud.

Modern machines transformed two adjoining dairy farms into Arcadia. The Farm, by contrast, is more like a homestead on the old American frontier.

Ilona also could be a visitor from the past. Middle-aged, with rough homespun clothing and black hair cut so short she could be a nun, she also looks more leathery than I remember. It's as if the Maine woods were turning her into pemmican.

She wastes no time. While we talk, she continues weeding the carrot beds. She addresses the plants, not me, as if the mere presence of an avatar was polluting the community.

"Is there anything you need? I could ask Zoltan to—"

"We are perfect," Ilona says.

"We've developed a new variety of blueberry that thrives in this weather," I say, in the spirit of gardeners trading tips.

"Blueberry!" Ilona snorts, as if I'd offered to send her some spare night soil.

"They have excellent antioxidant properties."

"This is no yuppie commune!"

I cast around in my mind for something else to offer. "We're thinking of getting a new printer. Once we do that, we could send Rupert over with the ones we're currently using. Then you could—"

"Printers? This is Zoltan's idea?"

"Actually, no, he..."

"That is why Zoltan say absolutely no, he doesn't want to come here to us. No playthings for him here."

"Well, Zoltan seems to enjoy Arcadia." I put some inflection on the word "seems" to see if it elicits any response. "He has his friends."

"Friends?" Ilona barks. "That is unusual. Only friends are his games."

"You know, he's quite brilliant."

"This is no age for geniuses." She holds up a handful of

weeds, without deigning to turn around. "This an age for hard work. For dirty hands."

"But if it weren't for Zoltan, Arcadia probably couldn't survive. It's because of his coding that—"

Ilona stands up, face reddening. Now she's looking at me, and her expression is terrifying. "Survive? Survive at what price?"

Memories of the conflict that led to the schism flood back when I hear the accusatory tone in her voice. "I know that we haven't always agreed, but—"

"Arcadia is armed compound." She spits this out as if it were a pebble in her porridge.

"It's a dangerous world, Ilona. We're not in the middle of nowhere like you."

"This is not nowhere. This is somewhere. You could have come here, too. With us. But you were just like Zoltan. You would not give up on your toys."

"My *toys*?" This is too much. "I don't have any toys. Are you are referring to my lab?"

She's not listening to me. It's as if I've intruded on a dramatic monologue that began long before my visit. "We must to start over again. Without the diseases of that world out there. In that soil. The spores. The root rot. The planet cannot be transformed with guns. That is the lesson of the history."

"You can't shut out the world. You have your connections, too. You have your VR."

"We don't kill!" Ilona is shouting. "And now you are

getting it back, yes? That is your urgent crisis, yes? Someone is attacking you. Of course!"

The conversation is going off the rails. I need to bring it back to Zoltan. I need to find out if she knows something about him that I don't.

"Yes, yes, someone is attacking us. And I... I need to know if Zoltan is doing his best at the moment. I think maybe his mind is elsewhere. Maybe he is thinking of coming here."

"Rubbish! He will never come here."

"Or maybe he is thinking that you will return to Arcadia."

"Are you listening, woman? We would never return to Arcadia. You are infected. All of you are contaminated. From very start, but I never saw it then. I was blind. So was Aladar. We did not see it."

"See what?"

"The infection."

"What infection?"

"I have work to do."

"What do you mean 'from the very start'?"

"You must go."

"Ilona, please, I still need—"

"You need nothing. You need to go. And you don't come back."

With that, she throws her weeds at my face.

I flinch. The weeds, of course, go right through me.

But the words stick.

Chapter Ten

I am back in my own greenhouses, weeding my own carrot beds and thinking about what happened ten years ago. Arcadia had already weathered the dispute over the Captures. I thought we'd become more cohesive as a result, just as when a bone heals after a fracture and becomes stronger. That's exactly how I put it at the meeting where we evaluated our decision to accept the Captures. Only much later did a more familiar and apt metaphor occur to me.

Once, during our 2016 expedition in Antarctica, when my team was crossing a stretch in the Allan Hills region we'd traversed many times before, the snowmobile just in front of me suddenly disappeared from view. I must have looked down for a moment to wipe my nose or check the odometer. When I looked up, Miguel was gone, swallowed by the ice. I quickly squeezed the brakes so I too would not fall into the crevasse. The six of us gingerly stepped off of our vehicles and crept up to the jagged hole to see if there was anything we could do for our poor colleague.

He had been lucky. He'd toppled onto a ledge as his snowmobile continued deeper into the fathomless darkness. His perch, however, was precarious, one leg hooked around a jagged outcropping of ice and the rest of him balanced on the narrow ledge. We attached a rope to the back of our most heavily loaded snowmobile and I, being the lightest, belayed down. Miguel had dislocated both shoulders and was barely conscious from a blow to the back of his head. I hugged him around the midsection and the machine pulled us up to safety.

We'd taken that same route many times to our research site. Convinced of its solidity, we had simply followed our own tracks, confident that the past was our most reliable guide. But that section must have been a vulnerable ice bridge that our repeated trips had fatally weakened. It could have been any of us. Life in the frostlands is precarious.

Our community, too, concealed hidden fractures. Arcadia had begun with singular purpose and unanimity about our general trajectory and the methods by which we would settle disagreements. That trajectory, however, assumed one thing: the relative stability of the world outside Arcadia's walls. Yes, we were prepared for the rising temperatures, for the disruptions to the power grid and the food shortages. We recoiled from the prospect of something worse. We had no intention of trying to ride out a nuclear war or a pandemic. Survivalists we were not.

It was the breakdown in order that we didn't anticipate,

the bandage of civilization peeling back from the festering wound of barbarous grievances. We scientists and poets and engineers and painters were ill equipped for one civil war, let alone many, or for the United States to break apart.

It was only later, when I had time to peruse books on American history in our library, that I discovered how precarious this country had always been. I was astounded to learn that the Founding Fathers had only conjured America into existence through an elaborate bait-and-switch in 1778, promising the original thirteen fractious states that they would merely update the Articles of Confederation and then instead engineering a constitution for a brand-new federal authority. This could be considered the third of a Holy Trinity of original sins, along with the genocide of Native Americans and the enslavement of Africans. The essential tension between the states and the federal government never really went away. It simmered and exploded in the blue-gray standoff of the Civil War. It resurfaced in the black-white conflict of the civil rights era. And it came back one last time with a vengeance in the great red-blue conflicts of the 2010s and 2020s.

E pluribus unum, out of many, one—that was the official slogan of the United States. But the *pluribus* never really reconciled themselves to the *unum*. They were just waiting for an excuse to rewind history: first reviving the racism of the twentieth century, then the military conflict of the nineteenth century, then the separately governed regions of the eighteenth century, and, finally, the tribalism of the very beginning. The entire history of the country flashed before its eyes in the last flickering moments of its demise.

Arcadia was the last place I imagined such conflicts would reproduce themselves.

The Horvaths were quiet, all three of them working without complaint and speaking to each other in Hungarian, a language no one else in the community understood. They were erratics, just like the rest of us. Erratics are the boulders that glaciers pick up at high altitudes and deposit down below as the ice melts away. Human history had plucked up all of us future Arcadians and transported us to our place of repose in northern Vermont. We were all from elsewhere. We were all misfits.

But the Horvaths were perhaps the oddest of all. They refused to take up arms when Arcadia suffered those initial attacks in the early 2030s. This was a do-or-die moment, as violent fanatics threatened to overrun our community. There was no room for negotiations. The attackers would have killed us all without hesitation—indeed, two of our number did succumb to their injuries. Armed resistance was truly the only option. But the Horvaths insisted on their pacifism. They were prepared for martyrdom. Fortunately, the rest of us were not. We put the Horvaths to work in the makeshift infirmary and turned our attention to beating back the wolves.

It's impossible to know how a person will respond in a crisis. Some of our more competent members simply shut down. Others I'd considered flaky turned out to be quiet heroines. Thus did Arcadia jump to a different path altogether, guided by those like Anuradha and me who reacted with resolve to save the community, while other Original Members took a step back, mortified by their lack of grace under pressure. In the chaos of the moment, the Horvaths' pacifism simply faded into the background, like any other philosophy that doesn't accord with ongoing revelation. They continued to go about their business, and I thought they'd accommodated themselves to the new reality.

What choice did they, or the rest of us, have? The world outside our walls was falling apart. The coastal cities of Miami and New Orleans were no more. The Great Oregon Tsunami of 2019 had rendered large sections of the Pacific Northwest uninhabitable. Certain parts of the country—the Republic of Western Massachusetts, the anarchic commonwealth of Northern California—functioned as more or less independent entities. The very rich had walled themselves off in luxurious underground compounds and mountain redoubts. The Pentagon still maintained military para-states in and around missile installations and critical energy infrastructure. The "federal government" based in Kansas City had little influence beyond the Midwest Perimeter and the archipelago of Pentagon outposts around the country. Everywhere else, chaos reigned. We were exceptionally lucky to live in Arcadia, and I thought that we were all committed to improving our lot incrementally.

When the break came, it took me completely by surprise. And because I wasn't paying attention, I nearly fell into the crevasse along with the rest of the community. The rebellion had been brewing for some time—how long, I never found out. At one point, during the summer of 2041, the Horvaths and their co-conspirators attempted, through discussion and passive resistance, to take over Arcadia. They failed, though not without attracting several more families to their side. Ultimately we voted to cast them out. This was not as cruel as it sounds. They didn't want to stay under anyone's rule other than their own. We supplied them with the food, materials, and even technology to start their own community. We even gave them Emily, our AI at the time, to escort them to the location of their proposed Farm.

Still, I didn't think they would survive. They turned down our offer of a hovercar. They insisted on walking two hundred miles across exceedingly dangerous terrain, as if determined to create their own trail of tears. After Emily let us know of their successful journey, I still gave them only the slightest chance of surviving their first year. Yet they did, even with the root rot, even through losing Emily in their second year, and Aladar's death when a tree toppled the wrong way.

Ilona said that the problem with Arcadia "had been there from the beginning." Was she rewriting history to justify the subsequent rebellion? Arcadia had not been armed in the early 2020s. None of us ever imagined then that guns would be necessary. We didn't anticipate that the world would crack so easily. For all the time I'd spent around ice and all my experience with the unpredictability of glaciers, I was still shocked at the calamitous course of human events. In what followed, we discovered new things about ourselves. As did the Horvaths—they just didn't talk about it with me.

Now I know that Zoltan isn't planning to help his mother take over Arcadia. The Farm has no such ambition, and he prefers our relative modernity. Still, I suspect some plan behind his plan, some genuine trajectory behind his feints. Although he clearly rejects the neo-Luddism of his parents, it's not clear that he has similarly rejected the post-modern option of CRISPR. Could he feel that he's hiding his light beneath a bushel at Arcadia when CRISPR could give him access to technology beyond compare?

I remain deeply skeptical of his plan to ally with the Movement. I'm not even sure the Movement exists. It could be no more than a rumor that reflects a desperate desire for meaningful opposition to CRISPR and the other corporate conglomerates. According to Zoltan's reports, the Movement is as ruthless in its methods as the forces it opposes. Or perhaps he's only in touch with scammers, or even some catfishing counterfeit of CRISPR.

For want of better, I'm grasping at the slenderest of straws—the possibility that my ex-husband is helping me from beyond the grave, offering me information that could bring down the house of CRISPR, a house built on sand. That's what Julian is telling me, and that only he can supply the means to destroy it.

I feel like one of those credulous Victorian biddies who

were convinced by charlatan mediums that they could communicate with their dearly departed husbands.

With a heavy heart, I prepare to go to Xinjiang for the next Ouija message from Julian.

Chapter Eleven

Transcript of conversation between Emmanuel Puig and Rachel Leopold,
Yinchuan City, December 16, 2051

Rachel Leopold: Did you find anything?

Emmanuel Puig: It's good to see you too.

Rachel: I'm sorry. I have to meet Gordon in five minutes.

Emmanuel: I thought you'd at least appreciate my avatar.

Rachel: It's a pleasure to finally talk with Albert Einstein. Now, did you find anything?

Emmanuel: In his report, no. Our IT department did its best. There's nothing there.

Rachel: I'm sorry to hear that.

Emmanuel: But there is something else.

Rachel: What?

Emmanuel: In the message you DM'ed me.

Rachel: Wait, don't tell me!

Emmanuel: You don't want to know?

Rachel: I *do* want to know. But we have to be careful.

Emmanuel: Remember, I'm Einstein. I've thought ahead. Our IT department wrote its interpretation on this piece of paper.

Rachel: Wait, don't—

Emmanuel: It's polarized in a way that only you can see it. Even I can't read it. It's keyed to the specific frequency of your avatar and yours alone.

Rachel: Really? Okay, show me what you've got.

Emmanuel: Does it make any sense?

Rachel: Yes, it makes a lot of sense.

Emmanuel: I'm glad that I can be of service. Now, if I could just ask you a few questions…

Rachel: I have to meet Gordon in a—

Emmanuel: Like I said, I'm preparing an annotated version of your husband's final report. I just have a few questions.

Rachel: Email them to me. I promise to get back to you.

Emmanuel: I would be most grateful!

Chapter Twelve

Gordon looks just like his father. If it weren't for that unnerving resemblance—which he tries to conceal beneath a beard covering his weak chin, hair flopping down over his broad forehead, and sunglasses that obscure his hooded eyes—I would be tempted to believe that he'd been swapped at birth. Gordon is nothing like Julian—or me. He has always been obsessed with one thing only: making money. In this regard he'd been a child prodigy, creating apps and moneymaking websites and then a whole empire built of nothing but virtual merchandise and financial speculation.

As a young man, Gordon went to China to double his fortune and watched it increase tenfold. Even when that country fell apart and he ended up in the splinter state of Ningxia, he profited from all the chaos. I honestly don't know how he did it. He could draw money out of thin air much as our little machines sucked carbon dioxide from the atmosphere, except that he didn't rely on chemistry or magic—just the sheer force of his will. I suppose he inherited his focus and determination from Julian. Even so, I don't really see any traces of my former husband in his personality. Julian was a plodding herbivore, chewing the cud of his few original observations. My older son is a bird of prey, always attentive to tiny movements in his field of vision that he can turn to his carnivorous advantage.

Though I've never visited Gordon in Ningxia, I've seen him quite regularly. He's rich enough to visit Arcadia every few years—in person, not just via VR. An armored personnel carrier brings him and his three well-armed bodyguards from the Montreal airport to our humble community. He comes across like some combination of distant potentate and shaman. While his guards camp outside our walls, he drags inside an immense shipping container of gifts—the latest devices for the kids, new medicines that aren't yet downloadable, cotton fabric to make into clothes. Then he stays up late regaling the community with tales of the heroes and villains of what were once the western reaches of China.

Now he's delighted to show me around Yinchuan City, the capital of Ningxia, even if only virtually.

"Aurora DM'ed to let me know to expect a visit," he says when we meet outside the Yinchuan Museum of Contemporary Art. "I've set up a dinner at our favorite restaurant. You can't eat anything even remotely like it in Arcadia. And you'll be able to meet Ming-hwa. She's eager to get to know you."

"I'm looking forward to it. Thank you for the hospitality, Gordon."

"As long as you downloaded that special program for your printer that I sent you, you should be able to get a close approximation of their lamb-and-cumin dish. It's really quite—"

"Didn't you bring something similar on your last visit?"

It hadn't looked special, just an array of freeze-dried cubes. Reconstituted, however, the cubes created a Uyghur feast, from lamb-and-ginger dumplings to Eight Treasure Tea. It fed all 250 of us.

"Oh, yes, of course. But that was just a taste. I want to give you the full experience. The music, the spectacle. Well, as much as you can get as an avatar."

Gordon is wealthy enough to enjoy real food three times a day. In fact, I don't think he's ever had to eat seaweed in any of its many permutations. He dresses in real leather and cotton. And he only travels by VR when air travel isn't feasible. He lives as if civilization continues to bring all the riches of the world within reach. Thus have the wealthy always lived outside of time.

Gordon walks me around the outside of the museum, a long white structure that hugs the nearby river.

"The architect said he wanted to imitate the waves of the Yellow River," Gordon explains, "and the rolling dunes of the desert."

It looks like three distinct piles of paper that some celestial thumb pressed down upon to create the undulations.

From what I can see in the distance, this is a city full of such odd creations: a huge tilted nautilus shell; a skyscraper with multiple towers like a candelabra; a tall, thin sheet of red, rippling glass. In Arcadia, form strictly follows function. I've become unaccustomed to such enormous wastes of money and creativity, the kinds of postmodern potlatches by which local oligarchs prove their worth and display their wealth. I fear that Gordon may be one of them. His thumbprint can probably be found everywhere in this city. I don't ask. I don't want to know.

"It's probably ridiculous to suggest, but I should mention that we'll soon be expanding Arcadia. I could possibly get you and Ming-hwa onto the list."

Gordon just laughs. "Really, Mom. I would shrivel up and die in Arcadia. I might as well join a lamasery."

I launch into a description of how Gordon could contribute to the development of Arcadia. It's a prepared speech, and it's all nonsense. Gordon and Arcadia are a terrible mismatch. During my deception, however, I DM him the same message I'd sent to Aurora. Unlike his sister, Gordon doesn't need any time to sift through his memories. I can see that he immediately understands what I'm looking for. It takes him no time at all to supply what I need.

"It's hopeless, Mom," Gordon cuts me off. "Remember when Dad tried to get me to help out with his big idea for the house in DC? He wanted to remodel the basement so that we could have a kitchen and dining room down there? He had this grand plan that we would do this project together and have some father-son bonding time. It just didn't work out. Same thing with you and Arcadia. It's just not a good fit. I'm sorry."

I've known ever since he was a child that Gordon is quick-witted, but I hadn't seen his intellect in action for a long time. His ability to pivot so smoothly, to refashion the nugget of information so that it seamlessly flowed into our conversation, was Gordon at his best. He'd come up with an anecdote about Julian instantaneously and established immediately that what he was about to say was patently false in a way that only I would know. After all, our home in Washington, the one destroyed in 2022 in Hurricane Donald, didn't have a basement.

"Ah, I guess you're right," I say admiringly. "You've always been a frontiersman, Gordon. In fact, I'm surprised you've acquired the trappings of domesticity here in Xinjiang. It must be Ming-hwa's influence."

"I'll let you be the judge of that," Gordon says, beckoning me down to a path along the river. "We can walk to the restaurant. You can see it from here, anchored to the riverbank. It's a facsimile of an imperial barge. Not very authentic, but the food is excellent. And it serves wine from my vineyard—an excellent Merlot."

I am torn. I want to meet Gordon's wife. They've been together for almost two years now. It's his third marriage, but the other two were so short-lived that I found out about them only after their dissolution. I'm understandably curious about what kind of person can tether a bird of prey.

But I also want to rush back to Arcadia with this new information. Along with the interpretation that Emmanuel Puig offered of the message sent to Aurora, I have a pretty good idea of what I need to do next.

I decide to compromise. I'll stay for the first course, be properly introduced to Ming-hwa, then beg off for the rest of the evening. Gordon will understand. The very fact that I, who rails so often against retinal implants, DM'ed him conveys the urgency of the situation.

I set off after Gordon. But something isn't right.

"Hey, Mom, we're going this way." Gordon is waving at me. "Down here. Toward me. Mom? Mom!"

I'm doing everything I'm supposed to do to move in Gordon's direction. But it isn't working. My son is getting smaller. It's as if someone has taken over the controls of the VR.

As it turns out, someone has.

Chapter Thirteen

I don't know where I am.

All I know is it's a desert. Undulating hills of sand stretch in every direction. I am on top of one of those hills, which affords me an unobstructed view of emptiness. No signs of habitation. No oasis in sight. No road or track of any kind cutting through the sand.

There are only three things in this landscape: me (or at least a version of me), the chair my avatar is sitting on, and an empty chair across from me.

It's midday. The sun, directly above my head, has burned a hole through the blue canvas of the sky.

One moment I was walking along that river away from my son and the next I'm sitting in this chair in the middle of an immense, barren expanse.

Here in the desert a limited range of avatar motion has been restored to me, but what use is it? Where can I go? I stand up, then sit down again. With a flick of my eyes I try to return to Arcadia. I can't. It's a bad dream from which I can't awaken.

As I search through screen after screen for some virtual way out of this desert, I become aware of a change in the landscape. A large man, or at least a large avatar, is now across from me. I'm overwhelmed by him even though we're both sitting down.

"Hello, Rachel," he says. "My apologies for bringing you to this meeting without any explanation. I didn't want to take you away from your son Gordon so suddenly, but we're on a rather tight schedule. You are, too, yes?"

"Where are we?"

"I hope you appreciate the view. It was quite a job to enable VR here, but it's worth it. What better place than the Sahara for a virtual rendezvous if you don't want to be interrupted?"

"I don't know who you are but—"

"I was a friend of your late husband. Well, 'friend' might be overstating the relationship. An acquaintance."

He's dressed in a black suit and a crisp white shirt, and that stirs a memory of something my ex-husband wrote in his report. He has a slight Australian accent, not a Russian one, but still I make a guess.

"You're Ivanov," I said. "Or at least that's what Julian called you. The man from CRISPR who interrogated him."

"Interrogated? I wouldn't use that word. We contracted with your husband to write a report, and then we asked him some questions about it. Everything was very professional.

On our side, at least."

"You tried to kidnap my younger son, my Benjamin, and you failed. I don't see how that was 'very professional.'"

"Well, your Benjamin was a very nettlesome fellow who was trying to destroy the planet. I know that sounds over the top, but honestly, he would have done it. Anyway, he cost us a lot of money, but that's not why I'm here. And that's not why you're here."

"I have no information for you."

"Oh, I wouldn't jump so quickly to that conclusion, Rachel. Please hear me out."

"Do I have a choice?"

"We all have choices. But we haven't gotten to your choice yet."

"Go on," I say weakly.

Ivanov places his hands on his large stomach, looking for all the world like a happy, expectant mother. "We know about your research. In rough outline. And we know that you are currently on some kind of quest. We don't really care about your quest, but we do care about your work."

"I'm just visiting my children."

"I didn't realize that Emmanuel Puig was one of your children. Perhaps another illegitimate son? Sorry, that was unnecessary."

I seethe. Puig had assured me that our meetings were entirely secure. "How do you know about my research?"

"We've been following your career for a very long time."

"I haven't had a career for a very long time."

"Indeed, your last publication on the ice-albedo effect was in 2021. *Journal of Glaciology*, volume twelve, number two. Top notch. Or so I've been assured by those who know their ice. But you have been in touch recently with Bjorn Amundsen. We've simply filled in the blanks. And now, suddenly, you're all over the map. So much travel at your age must be taxing."

"I don't know if I'll have another opportunity to see my family."

"Precisely. And that brings us to the crux of the matter. Your choice."

"This, too, is just a conversation, not an interrogation, right?"

"Not even a conversation, really. Just a chat."

"In the Sahara. Against my will."

Ivanov shrugs. "If that's how you feel, I won't keep you long. Here's your choice. You can hand over all of your research results and we will, in exchange, give you the same drug we promised your late husband. It will extend your life as much as forty years and, given subsequent medical advances, probably a great deal longer. We'll also throw in a supply for Gordon and Aurora and your grandchildren, because we believe in family at CRISPR International. Without family, we are nothing."

"How thoughtful."

"Or we can go about it the hard way. We'll take your research results by force. And I think you know that we are fully capable of that."

"In a professional way, I'm sure."

"When the fate of the earth hangs in the balance, we must act by all means necessary. Which is why we are making this generous offer to you."

"What's the point of extending my own life and the life of my family if the planet shrivels up and dies?"

"But it won't. We've run the numbers. Many times. Barring something unexpected, like our life-extension drug falling into too many hands, the planet will regain its equilibrium in about four hundred years. After it jettisons approximately 99 percent of the human population."

"And you'll be part of the 1 percent."

"And you can be, too."

If I could have spit in his face, I would have. "I'm not interested in individual longevity. I care only about species longevity."

"So do we, so do we," Ivanov says, clapping his hands together like a small child. "We are truly on the same page."

"We're not even in the same book."

"Oh, but we are! We're just quibbling about the numbers. We both want humanity to survive these difficult times. One percent of humanity is still a lot of humanity."

"Somehow I don't think that these difficult times are quite as difficult for you and your colleagues as they are for everyone else."

"We all have a strong tribal instinct. You want your family to survive and prosper, yes? You want Arcadia to survive and prosper, yes? If you agree to our terms, you can ensure their safety. Their *sustainability*."

"I'm an old woman and I'm tired," I tell him, thinking that I'm overusing this excuse. "Do I have to make this decision right now? Under this hot sun in the middle of a desert?"

"Of course not. You have twenty-four hours. It's a pleasure to finally meet you, Rachel. I've admired you from a distance."

And with that, Ivanov disappears. I sit in my chair for a moment, relieved that I don't have to make an immediate decision. But I fear that Ivanov is giving me time, not space—that I will have to sit in this chair for the next twenty-four hours.

Before this fear can take proper hold over me, however, the desert is gone and I'm back in Arcadia.

Chapter Fourteen

I remove the VR headset and discover Zoltan standing in front of me.

"I was visiting Gordon," I begin.

"Emergency meeting of the Council," he says tersely.

I look down at my wristband. It has turned orange.

"What's happening?"

"Code breakers," Zoltan says, helping me out of the VR apparatus. "Rupert found two units operating in parallel next to the outer perimeter."

"CRISPR?"

"That's my guess."

"Can you change the locks again?"

"The units would immediately know the new code."

"How much time do we have?"

"If they were ordinary computers, we would have at least seventy-five years. But these are some new type of quantum computers."

"So how much time do we have?"

Zoltan looks sheepish. That's when I know how serious the situation is: Zoltan never looks sheepish. "Possibly as little as twenty-four hours."

"And what about the inner perimeter? It has a different code, right?"

"Yes. They might try to decrypt it, or they might use brute force."

I can't resist asking him: "If you knew then what you know now, would you have breached the outer perimeter?"

He clears his throat, but then says nothing. And that's even more unusual.

I find Arcadia in a tightly wound spiral of anxiety. Everyone is conferring, but in whispers, as if afraid of waking someone or something. Defense corps members have taken up arms but are not yet at their guard posts. Zoltan says that they've only been told that an attack similar to the one we experienced the day before might happen again. We have to avoid a panic.

The Council meeting is already a pitched battle of accusations and recriminations when Zoltan and I arrive.

"This is what we warned you about," Bertrand is saying, his eyes flicking toward Zoltan and me. "If we allied with the Movement against CRISPR, then CRISPR would attack us."

"As far as we can tell," Zoltan says above the uproar, "the bots left the units during yesterday's attack. In fact, I now suspect that it was simply a distraction while they put those units in place. Which means it was something they did *before* we decided to work with the Movement."

"Then why are they doing this?" asks Bertrand.

Zoltan skirts the question. "I'm trying as hard as you are to understand what's going on."

Other Council members begin to talk again. Anuradha has to stand to quiet the tumult. "Let's not focus on the past. The question is: What should we do now? Zoltan, please update us on any cooperation with the Movement."

Zoltan clears his throat. "I made contact with the Movement representative yesterday and provided the data we were able to gather during the breach. He said it was invaluable."

"How invaluable?" asks Bertrand. "Invaluable enough to disrupt CRISPR's attack?"

Zoltan purses his lips. "I'm still waiting to hear back."

The other Council members are abuzz with questions. They want to know what to expect, how long the outer perimeter wall can hold, what kind of weapons we might be facing. They want to know about any emergency contingency plans.

Above all, they want to know what CRISPR's looking for.

I bang the table with my fist. That gets their attention. Startled, they look at me. They've never seen me act this way.

I say simply, "CRISPR wants me."

Chapter Fifteen

Rupert and Karyn are sitting cross-legged on the floor of the laundry room. Karyn is drawing circles on a piece of paper. Petting his rabbit, Rupert is watching carefully.

"Do you see that, Rachel?" he asks when I come in. "Karyn draws perfect circles every time. I wish I had that kind of hand-eye coordination."

"I can teach you," Karyn offers.

"No, you can't," Rupert says without a trace of self-pity. "I can do many things. But I will never be able to do that."

"What have you two been up to?" I ask, genuinely curious. Since Karyn was released from quarantine, she and Rupert have become inseparable.

"Karyn doesn't have access to any of our digital resources," Rupert says. "I've been telling her the story of Arcadia so she can create a graphic novel about our community."

"Is that something you want to do?" I ask Karyn.

"I like to draw. But I also like welding."

"We don't need any spot-welding at the moment," Rupert says. "But we don't have any graphic novels about Arcadia."

Karyn looks at him with what seems almost like affection. "I would like to help you better understand yourselves."

Lizzie has repurposed Karyn to help the community in whatever ways she can. Her original programmed abilities—to collect information, to pluck drones from midair—might also come in handy at some point. The jury is still out on her cartooning capabilities.

"Thank you, Karyn," I say. "On a somewhat different topic, what can you tell me about CRISPR International?"

"CRISPR International began operations in 2020 and quickly established a reputation as a leader in bioengineered medical solutions. It has since diversified into many fields of innovation."

"Have you ever had any contact with CRISPR International?"

"No," Karyn says.

"None at all?" I press.

"There are no CRISPR operations in Canton, Ohio."

It's impossible to get an AI to deviate from its core narrative, but it's always worth a try.

"Rupert, I want to ask you about CRISPR as well. Can you pull up a map of its facilities in Darwin, Australia?"

"Of course, Rachel. I'm looking at it now."

"How many buildings are there?"

"Four."

"They differ in size, yes?"

"I can give you their square footage in descending rank."

"Is one quite a bit smaller than the other three?"

"The smallest building is 14,763 square feet. The other three are all larger than 35,983 square feet."

"Can you tell me the purpose of this smallest building?"

"The other three buildings are clearly research facilities, given the energy requirements and the nature of the effluents. The smallest building does not have a research function."

"If you had to guess, what would you say that its function is?"

"There is an 86 percent probability that it has an executive function."

"How many floors does it have?"

"Three floors above ground. One floor below ground."

"Can you tell me what takes place in this basement?"

"I am sorry, Rachel, I do not know."

But I'm relieved that the coded messages from my former husband make sense. From Aurora, I learned that I was looking for the smallest of four things; Emmanuel Puig confirmed that the CRISPR headquarters in Darwin consisted of four buildings; and Gordon pointed me in the direction of the basement. Julian wanted someone—perhaps me—to know what was going on in the basement of the smallest of the four CRISPR buildings in Darwin. Perhaps it's the nerve center of the corporation. Perhaps my husband anticipated this very moment, when CRISPR International would try to breach the outer perimeter of Arcadia. Perhaps if I can get into that basement, I can flip a remote kill switch on these code-breaking units. Perhaps I can bring down the edifice of CRISPR with a great crash. I'm putting a lot of faith in a string of conjectures that could collapse as easily as a fragile ice bridge.

I put my hand on Rupert's shoulder. It's as soft as human flesh beneath his threadbare flannel shirt. "You found the code-breaking units just outside the outer perimeter."

"Yes, Rachel."

"How long until they break through?"

"Somewhere between 8 and 8.5 hours."

"Can they be disabled?"

"They are hardened. And attached to the outer perimeter. They can't be destroyed without either turning off the perimeter wall or destroying it."

"And what will happen after the outer perimeter is breached?"

Rupert looks at his rabbit. "I do not know."

"Tell me, both of you, how you feel about the extinction of the human race."

Rupert is the first to respond. "The extinction of the human race would mean the end of Arcadia. That is unacceptable."

Karyn adds, "I am a human being. I do not want to witness the extinction of our species."

I'm astonished. "Excuse me?"

Karyn repeats, word for word, what she'd just said.

"You never said anything before about being human."

"No one asked me."

This is a violation of the protocols: AIs are supposed to know that they are AIs. I gently point out, "You have capabilities that greatly exceed those of a human being."

"I am happy to teach you these capabilities," Karyn responds.

"Rupert, can you explain to Karyn what she is?"

Rupert provides a concise summary of her manufacture.

"Rupert is mistaken," Karyn says when he is done. "I was born in Canton, Ohio, twenty-five years ago. I can draw you pictures of my parents, if you like."

I'm flummoxed. "But, Karyn, why don't you eat or drink anything?"

Karyn freezes. Then she begins to hit herself in the forehead. Once. Twice. Three times, with increasing force.

"Wait, Karyn," I say. "You must be on a diet!"

Karyn stops. "Yes, that's right. I am on a diet."

I don't have time to explore this existential issue any further. If Rupert isn't bothered by the contradiction, then I won't be either. But it's the strangest bug we've ever come across in an AI.

"Rupert, what if I told you that, in four hundred years, only 1 percent of the human race will survive?"

Rupert calculates. "That would be eighty million people. If evenly distributed over the earth's surface, they would not likely survive. But if concentrated in sustainable communities like Arcadia, the human race could continue at those levels."

"But the loss of 99 percent of humanity would be greater than any genocide that has taken place on this planet."

"For humans," Rupert agrees. "But during the Permian-Triassic extinction event..."

"Yes, I know, Rupert," I interrupt him. "Do you see any value whatsoever in trying to save any portion of that 99 percent?"

Rupert looks at me in his unblinking way. "I can tell from the timbre of your voice, Rachel, that you care about saving some portion of that 99 percent, even though you would not know the vast majority of them. If you care about saving them, then I care about saving them."

I turn to Karyn. "And what do you think?"

"I think it would make a good story. *Saving the 99 Percent*: That would be the title of a very interesting graphic novel."

That's about as much as I can expect from them.

"Okay, then." I lower myself with some difficulty to the floor and sit cross-legged between them. I take out a pen and begin to turn the perfect circle that Karyn has drawn into a map. "Here's my plan."

Chapter Sixteen

Transcript of conversation between Emmanuel Puig and Rachel Leopold, Buenos Aires, December 17, 2051

Rachel Leopold: You were wrong!

Emmanuel Puig: Probably. I'm wrong about a lot of things. That's why I wanted to get your feedback on these annotations.

Rachel: I'm not talking about your annotations. I'm talking about this. Our meetings. They're not secure.

Emmanuel: My IT people assured me that—

Rachel: They were wrong. Are you working for CRISPR International?

Emmanuel: Of course not. As you well know, I'm the director of the World Geo-Paleontology—

Rachel: Have you ever received any funding from CRISPR?

Emmanuel: Not that I know of.

Rachel: Are you giving any information to CRISPR?

Emmanuel: Never.

Rachel: Why should I trust you?

Emmanuel: I'm a geo-paleontologist, just like your husband was. I've worked in the field for more than two decades. But presumably you know all this.

Rachel: Let me ask again: Why should I trust you?

Emmanuel: Your children trust me. They've already shared a great deal of information with me about your husband. And I've kept all that information in confidence. Even from you.

Rachel: That's not much to pin my hopes on.

Emmanuel: What I want more than anything, Rachel, is your report. And your help with my annotations. I would not do anything that would jeopardize that.

Rachel: I am reassured by your appeal to self-interest, and I need your help. But I just don't know if you'll turn around and betray me. Or if you already have.

Emmanuel: Okay, let me think. How about this: I have been in touch with your youngest son, with Benjamin. But I haven't given that information to anyone.

Rachel: Why were you in touch with Benjamin?

Emmanuel: Fact-checking my annotations.

Rachel: That's absurd. I don't believe you. My son has been underground for decades.

Emmanuel: He told me that you once forbade him from playing something called "paintball" with his friends because you thought the game was too violent.

Rachel: Yes, okay, I remember that. And a fat lot of good it did, too. But I can't believe that Benjamin would put himself at risk for something as trivial as fact-checking your annotations on Julian's manuscript.

Emmanuel: Well, he also needed something from me. I am well connected here in Buenos Aires.

Rachel: What did he need in Argentina?

Emmanuel: I can't tell you.

Rachel: He's my son. You can tell me.

Emmanuel: Number one, he told me in confidence, and I would never betray that confidence. Number two, you've already said that these discussions are insecure.

Rachel: Okay, then, maybe I can trust you. I'm in a hurry. This will have to be a leap of faith. I'm going to DM you some coordinates. Can your IT people help me?

Emmanuel: Let me disconnect for a moment to find out. ...Okay, they tell me that those coordinates are for a secure location. It's password protected.

Rachel: Can you help me bypass that password protection?

Emmanuel: That would be illegal.

Rachel: It could potentially save the planet.

Emmanuel: I meet a lot of people who believe that they can save the planet. Can you give me any further information?

Rachel: No. These are not secure discussions. You'll have to take my word for it. Just as I have taken your word.

Emmanuel: Well, I can't help you.

Rachel: You are such an academic. All talk. No action.

Emmanuel: But I know someone who can help you. Someone I think you can trust.

Chapter Seventeen

We meet in Allan Hills.

Once upon a time that's where I took ice core samples, an hour by plane from the old McMurdo Station. We drilled through the dense blue ice of Antarctica during the day, and at night we listened as the fierce winds tried without success to uproot our tents. That wind was both bane and blessing. Sometimes it would force us to cancel the day's work because we couldn't get to the drill site by snowmobile, and during that time immense snowdrifts would cover our equipment. It created sastrugi, waves of hard-packed snow, that were hell to traverse. But the wind was also our friend, for over time it had swept away the surface ice, enabling us to dig even deeper into time.

On my final trip in 2018, we spent two months on the ice. Just before flying back to McMurdo, we succeeded in recovering a two-million-year-old sample. Trapped as bubbles in the ancient ice was air just as old, which showed us how the chemical composition of the atmosphere had changed over time. I brought this astounding information to Congress in what would be my last appearance. They looked at me as if I were just another mad scientist.

"That's a lot of cold air," one of the politicians quipped, and the rest of them took that as a signal to end the discussion.

Today the blue ice of Allan Hills is worn thin, revealing here and there the rocky, lunar landscape beneath. Once Antarctica contained 90 percent of all the ice on the planet. Millions of years have melted away in the span of decades. The weather is still inhospitable, the wind still fierce. There's really not much to see anymore, so no one visits on virtual excursions, even though it has been VR-enabled for some time. It is as barren as the desert, which technically it is, because there is still so little rainfall in this part of the continent.

Benjamin and I are alone.

I haven't seen my youngest son in decades. In his senior year of high school, he ran off to fight Islamic fundamentalists in Syria. He's been operating in a paramilitary netherworld ever since. At one point, my husband and I were informed that he'd been killed. But I never gave up hope. Even when more reliable reports surfaced of his continued activities under the *nom de guerre* Abu Jibril, I had to make do with a couple of blurry photos and cryptic thirdhand messages. He was as intangible to me as an avatar.

And now here he is, a real, live, only slightly less

intangible avatar. I'm not even sure if this is what he looks like. There is only a vague suggestion in the lineaments of the face of the teenage Benjamin I remember so well. But I'm probably just projecting my own feelings onto this computer-generated image, given how little I really know about my son—what he looks like, what he's doing, where he lives. It's only thanks to Emmanuel Puig that I was able to contact him at all. Puig left a message at a confidential drop, a place Benjamin had established for emergencies. I had no idea where I would go when I put on my VR headgear again, and I was pleasantly surprised to recognize the Allan Hills.

"Thank you for choosing this location," I tell him.

"I still remember your stories about this place," he says in a voice so much deeper than what I remember. "I'm only sorry that I can't see it the way you saw it."

I point to the snow-capped hills in the distance. "It was once all like that, different shades of white and black and blue. It was beautiful and desolate."

"And now it's just desolate."

"I can't tell you how many times I imagined this moment, you and me, this reunion. But never under these circumstances."

"I hope we can see each other in the flesh someday," Benjamin says.

I hope so, too, but I'm doubtful. Our lives are precarious, mine because of my age and his because of his vocation. The Fates, who have measured out the threads of our lives, can apply the scissors at any moment.

"I don't think either of us has much time," I say, clamping down on my emotions. "So perhaps we should focus on the problem at hand. We're safe? Really safe?"

"I wouldn't still be alive if I couldn't make sure that conversations like these are beyond the surveillance capabilities of the most sophisticated technology."

"I can't even begin to imagine what you've gone through over the years."

"We've all had our hardships." Benjamin is dismissive, but also probably still resentful over the role I played so many years ago in trying to prevent him from running off to war. "Are you well, Mother? Is that what this emergency is really about?"

"I'm fine. I'm trying to crack a code, something your father devised. Did he send you any strange messages? He sent one each to Aurora and Gordon."

"He sent me no messages, strange or otherwise."

That throws me for a loop. I'd expected a triad. I thought Benjamin would give me some final key to Julian's code. "Nothing at all?"

"He had no way of contacting me. After he blew my cover in Botswana, we made sure to sever all ties with him, and of course he died shortly afterward. Pretty much in the same place as those coordinates Emmanuel sent me."

"I'd hoped that you would know what to do when I get there. That you would supply the missing piece of the puzzle."

"I'm sorry to disappoint. Are you absolutely sure you want to VR there?"

"Your father must have thought it important enough if he sent me coded messages about it in his last moments."

"It's not safe to make an unauthorized trip inside CRISPR International, even for an avatar."

"Do you have any idea what I'll find there?"

Benjamin shakes his head. "But if they find you, they can hijack your system."

"I've already experienced that."

"They can kill you."

"You mean they can kill my avatar. Judi Dench won't mind."

"No, Mother, they can kill *you*. Directly. Administer a massive shock to your neural pathways. Cause a stroke."

"I guess that's just a risk I'll have to take."

"We can send one of our own in your place."

"No, it has to be me."

"Or you can wait."

"For?"

"The Movement."

"And what do you know about the Movement?"

"I *am* the Movement."

And I know instantly that this is no overstatement.

As we walk over the rocky ground and watch the winds, those still-fierce winds, swirl around us, Benjamin updates me on what he's been doing for the last ten years. I knew that he had abandoned his guerrilla warfare against the Caliphate and its subsequent incarnations once they became less virulent. I knew that he'd somehow acquired a dose of the same drug that Ivanov had first offered my husband and then tried to bribe me with. Benjamin now tells me that his threat to make this life-extension drug universally available for download forced CRISPR International to the negotiating table. There, he traded the precious dose for the release of dozens of life-saving biocures on which CRISPR had been making extraordinary profits for decades. Their distribution, free of charge, ended the suffering of tens of millions. It also filled the coffers of the Movement with donations from those who could afford to do so.

"What's the point of an eternal-life drug if poor people all over the world are dying from easily preventable diseases like malaria and TB?" Benjamin asks.

"No point at all, unless you're counting on those poor people dying anyway from drought or hunger or some other climate-related cause."

"They had their hidden agenda and we had ours," he admits. "We've brought together the finest hackers in the world to shut down CRISPR. We just needed some more information about their digital thumbprint."

Something clicks. "You contacted Zoltan. You asked him to allow that breach of the outer perimeter."

"He wasn't initially convinced. But, yes, he agreed in the end."

"Then why haven't you shut down CRISPR yet? You

know they're trying to break into Arcadia."

"Frankly, it's a race. We're using all of our computing power to crack their codes, and they're using all of theirs to crack yours."

I was angry. "But there's no risk to you at all!"

"Mother, everyone in the Movement is at great risk. We recognize the importance of Arcadia. And the importance of your research."

"You know nothing about my research."

"Actually, I know a great deal about it."

Now I was furious. "Zoltan had no right to divulge that information!"

"Your research is more important than any pledge of confidentiality. Tell me, if we were to help you VR to that geolocation and you were again to fall into the hands of CRISPR, would that be the end of the line? Could they effectively destroy your research project by destroying you? I'm sorry to be so blunt, but I need to know."

"No, my research will survive me." Even though he's my son, I'm reluctant to provide him with any more information. "Unless CRISPR decrypts our security codes first. How close are you?"

"Close." He pauses, looks at something in the middle distance. He's checking his updates. "But they too are close to penetrating your outer perimeter. Probably they're prepositioning some very sophisticated nanoweapons."

"Then I need to get back. But first send me to Darwin."

"I've told you, it's very dangerous and—"

"Benjamin." I'm having difficulty suppressing my emotions. I make one final effort. "I'm your mother. I don't know if we'll ever see each other again. Don't refuse what might be my final request."

Benjamin pauses, and I'm worried that something has gone wrong with the VR technology. But then he puts his right hand over his heart and bows his head slightly. "In the end, perhaps we are not so very different. Goodbye, Mother, and good luck."

Chapter Eighteen

I am half-convinced that, despite his promise, Benjamin will try to prevent me from embarking on my mission to Darwin. It would be fitting revenge for the attempt his father and I made so many years ago to stop him from running off to Syria to become a guerrilla. When I close my eyes on Allan Hills and then open them again, I fear I will find myself back in Arcadia's VR cubicle.

But no—I'm in a dark hallway. The only illumination comes from a few small lights inset in the walls at intervals just above the carpet. The corridor is empty. I check the coordinates. I pull up the 3D map. I'm reassured: It's Darwin. Because I've timed my visit for three in the morning, I see and hear nothing. My screens verify that I'm alone.

I am in the basement of the smallest of the four buildings in CRISPR International's complex. At some point, my husband was in this very basement and saw something important enough that he couldn't tell me via avatar, when we met at Arcadia just before he died. He must have known that CRISPR had him under complete surveillance. Instead, he embedded a code in messages to our two oldest children. He also knew something about Benjamin's capabilities and perhaps anticipated that our youngest would complete the puzzle by transporting me safely to this place. Julian was always proud of his prophetic vision, something I never genuinely appreciated until now.

The problem is that I'm not sure what I'm looking for. I increase the luminosity to see better as I navigate the basement's murk. Various closed doors lead off the corridor. If I were an expert at this technology, I could jump from the corridor into these adjoining rooms. Or perhaps, given the encrypted nature of the building, I'd just get ejected and end up back in the Allan Hills. I only hope that my husband anticipated my poor VR skills and that whatever he wants me to see will be obvious: a kill switch that says "don't touch" or an unsecured screen that lets me into the virtual heart of CRISPR. But that would be absurdly easy, and by definition nothing about CRISPR is easy.

At the end of the corridor is a glass wall with doors cut into it. Through it I can see a long oval table in what looks like a conference room, which probably explains why I can VR here in the first place. The technology was initially perfected to bring far-flung participants together for meetings.

There's nothing in the conference room. But as I turn around to retrace my steps, I see something.

It's a scale model of a set of buildings. At first I think it's a model of the complex I'm in, that the little white cubes correspond to CRISPR International's headquarters here in Darwin.

But when I move closer, I see the little cylindrical tower. It's a silo. I'm looking down at a miniature Arcadia.

It makes sense. At this very moment, CRISPR is bringing in its nanoartillery for a final assault on my community. The corporate executives probably use this model in their meetings to show what the prize looks like and where my research lab is located. They must have been planning this raid for more than a year—otherwise, my husband would never have seen this model in the first place.

But as I examine it more closely, I notice something odd. The building that houses my research lab isn't there. At first I wonder whether this is some future model of Arcadia after my lab has been expunged from history, a community that CRISPR has taken over for its own malign purposes. Then I notice that it lacks all the recent additions: the science center, the second set of greenhouses, even the stand-alone schoolhouse we built twenty years ago.

I'm not looking at our present or future. I'm looking at the *original* Arcadia.

Above the model is a set of photographs. I recognize the scenes. They are of the building of our community—the retrofitting of the original farm buildings, the construction of the Assembly Hall, the ribbon cutting. I amplify my resolution. Yes, there I am in the last picture, standing beside Anuradha, our arms around each other's waists. We look radiant. Ah, to be middle-aged again!

But there's one last picture—of the scale model resting on the table in what looks like the nearby conference room. A semicircle of people peers down at it as if it were a newborn child. They have their arms around each other's shoulders, and they're smiling.

This, I realize, is not a picture from the present. These CRISPR functionaries are dressed as if from the 2020s. All except one of them.

She's wearing a sari. And I recognize her.

I feel faint. I want to throw up. I move backward, dazed. Then I see what I'd first missed because I had been so focused on the scale model. Above the photograph is an inscription on the wall. It reads in bold black letters: *Arcadia, Our Future.*

I'm not thinking. I just want to run away from this horrible vision. I'm trying to move but I can't. I'm frozen in place.

Then Ivanov appears, a large slab of virtual flesh that now blocks what I've just seen but not really taken in.

"So you have discovered our secret," he says.

"I don't understand," I mumble.

"Of course you don't."

"I don't want to know," I add, though I already know far too much.

"It's quite simple," he says with relish. "We created Arcadia as an experiment in living."

"Don't. Don't tell me more."

"We could run our computer simulations and gather terabytes of information, but nothing beats a real live test."

I'm taking in large breaths of air between my sentences to quell the urge to vomit. "Everything we've done? All our struggles and successes? We were just rats in your maze?"

"I wouldn't choose that analogy. You were the proto-type. And it isn't for me or for CRISPR. It's for humanity. Arcadia is the future. It's how the surviving 1 percent will live. All those multibillionaire survivalists and their prepper bunkers back in the 2020s? They barely lasted a decade. You, however, have managed to solve the problem of sustainability. Well, with a little help."

"What help?"

"Where do you think all those fancy weapons came from back in 2032?"

"But Anuradha said—" I stop.

"Exactly. It would have been silly to end our experiment simply because of some voracious wolves. Ultimately, however, the attacks were quite useful. We needed to see if you could survive to the next generation and hand over power without going backward, like those foolish Hungarians and their—"

"I don't want to hear any more."

"And now we are preparing to establish Arcadias on every continent. Staffed by *our* people, but according to the blueprint that you and your fellow Arcadians have drawn up over the years. You should be very proud of your accomplishments."

My mind is racing. "But why are you attacking us?"

"Because of you, Rachel. Because of your research. You could ruin everything. You're not about to save the world. You're about to destroy it. We can't all live on the planet. Not if some of us are going to live forever. If climate change didn't exist, we'd have to invent it. Such an efficient, organic solution to the problem of overpopulation. Hats off to you, Mother Nature."

"But if Anuradha is your... your..." I can't bring myself to say it. My friend. My colleague. My role model!

"She has been a most invaluable employee. Imagine giving up your career to devote yourself to this experiment. We call her the astronaut. She traveled to the distant planet of Arcadia. But that planet has now spun out of her control. You have another generation that is pushing for a conflict with us."

"If you created Arcadia, why can't you just—" I'm too nauseated to continue.

"Just waltz right in through the back door? Well, we never imagined you would develop such sophisticated defenses. It's like dealing with a teenage son's rebellion, don't you think? You're so proud that he's so smart and independent. But then he uses all these new skills to defy you. We thought about bringing Zoltan in on the secret. Perhaps we should have. We might have avoided the current mess. But we still can, of course. *You* can."

I want to leave. But I can't move.

Ivanov is consulting his watch. "Your twenty-four hours

is almost up. Have you come to a decision, Rachel?"

I can't think. I don't want to think.

"Say the word, Rachel, and we will call off the attack."

"You are evil," I manage.

"We're both trying to save humanity," Ivanov says. "We're both on the side of the angels."

All along I'd thought of Arcadia as a Walden Three, a utopia established by scientists and artists who believed in common sense, not behaviorism or some other cultish ideology. We were pragmatists. Even when we disagreed about the Capture policy, we came to a decision in the old Vermont tradition of town meetings. We were the anti-Splinterlands, the place where compromise was still possible, where the middle had not been devoured by the extremes. To learn that our bold, democratic experiment in sustainability has been the plaything of a malevolent force leaves me completely disoriented. I have nowhere to turn, no polestar to guide me.

"Your decision, Rachel?"

We made difficult choices at every step. We took up arms. We killed. Even the terrible decisions were ultimately acceptable because they were *our* decisions. We believed that we were autonomous, that we were the architects of our own fate. And that proved to be the most durable illusion of them all.

"Rachel?"

I come to a decision. "Listen," I begin, and then he's gone and my decision has been made for me.

Chapter Nineteen

I am looking into Lizzie's eyes as she rapidly ushers me out of the VR apparatus.

"How?" That's all I can manage.

"I unplugged you," she says. "I'm sorry if I interrupted anything important."

"You didn't know? About Ivanov? About Darwin?"

"I don't know what you're talking about," she says quickly. "I'm here because we need you."

And now I notice that she's glowing green. I look down at my wrist: the band is red.

"They broke through the outer perimeter," I say.

"We need everyone. I was running past this room and saw that someone was using the equipment, so I unplugged you."

"Anuradha—" I begin.

"Don't worry, she's fine. She's helping Zoltan. You need to get to your post. You need to help my father."

"It's more important that I talk to Anuradha."

"It's a firefight out there, Rachel. We need you behind a gun. And I have to get back to my screens."

"Can they break through the inner perimeter?" I ask her.

She doesn't even turn around to answer.

Instead of going to my station to help Bertrand, I head for the Assembly Hall. As I push myself on aching joints as fast as I can speed-walk, I note the green outlines of my fellow Arcadians—standing, kneeling—their weapons half in and half outside the inner perimeter. What I see beyond the perimeter wall is too terrible to contemplate. Drones darken the midafternoon sky like a thick, low-lying cloud, and they're not small. They look like manta rays, with sinuous wings. Their two "eyes," where the cephalic fins would be, glow a dark red. The volley of energy from those eyes makes our perimeter wall shimmer, subtly distorting what I can see beyond. Our automatic defenses have been overwhelmed and we've fallen back on our own force of arms, using updated versions of the same weapons our enemy originally provided us. But this, too, seems like a losing battle. Every time we strike down one of the deadly creatures, another takes its place.

I turn away in fear and rush into the Assembly Hall. One more defender at the parapet probably wouldn't add much, but I don't know what my confrontation with Anuradha will do, either.

They are both in the Hub. Zoltan's hands are moving

frenetically in front of his screens. He's so absorbed in his efforts that he doesn't even notice my entrance. Anuradha is talking with several volunteers too young to shoulder weapons.

"The kitchen is preparing boxes—water, dried fruit," she's saying. "Put them in your wheelbarrows. Start at Section A. One of you work clockwise, the other counterclockwise."

She sends them scurrying past me. Several more wide-eyed young volunteers await their orders. But, seeing the look on my face, Anuradha takes my arm and escorts me out of the office. Perhaps she's expecting me to collapse in the face of crisis and is preparing to buck me up.

"Let's not distract Zoltan," she says. "Don't worry, Rachel, we can do this."

We're standing in an alcove just outside the assembly room. Through the windows in the doors, I can see that it has been turned into a makeshift hospital.

Anuradha follows my line of sight. "No one's been hurt yet. Except for Jackson, who dropped a gun on his toe."

"What were you thinking?" I ask. "All those years ago?"

She looks at me. "Thinking? When?"

"When you volunteered to set up Arcadia for CRISPR International. When you volunteered to be the serpent in our Garden of Eden."

She doesn't bother to pretend. I can see now how tired she is, how discouraged, how pessimistic. She takes a moment to formulate her response, then says, "I believe in

Arcadia just as much as you do. More now than ever."

"You can make them stop," I say.

"But I can't. I don't have any say with them. Not anymore. I send reports. I hear nothing back."

"Then send them another message. An urgent message."

"Trust me, I have. It's like praying for years and then losing your faith because no one responds."

Trust me, she says. I just shake my head.

"How did you find out?" she asks in a near-whisper.

"It doesn't matter."

"I'm not a spy, Rachel. My mission was to create a successful and sustainable community. Nothing more, nothing less. I have devoted my life to Arcadia."

I'm not sure if she's telling me the truth. I'm not sure if she even knows what the truth is anymore.

"And what will happen if these old 'friends' of yours breach the inner perimeter?"

Anuradha begins to cry, something I've never seen before. "I don't know that, either. I don't, Rachel. Please stop looking at me that way. I was just trying to do my best. To save the earth. To save people."

"To save *some* people."

She makes every effort to stop her tears. "It's a ship, Rachel, the earth is a ship. A sinking ship. And Arcadia is a lifeboat. I reached out to you. I wouldn't have left you behind. Please, you must believe me. My loyalties are only to Arcadia. To Arcadia and to you."

I have nothing more to say to her. I can't even tell where

her loyalties lie. Soon they'll be tested, though. I leave her weeping outside a room that, in hours or perhaps minutes, might be filled with the injured and the dying.

I feel old, hollowed-out, jetlagged from my VR journeys, at the end of my tether. I'm limping, though I don't remember hitting my leg against anything or pulling a muscle. I make it over to Section A, keeping my eyes on the ground so I don't have to look at what's attacking us. It's a childish gesture, but I feel as scared and lonely as a child right now.

Bertrand is standing at the earthworks, his weapon resting on top of the cistern. A box of fruit and water is by his foot, unopened. He's alone. My weapon is leaning against the tin shed. I grab it and take my position next to him. I begin to fire at the mantas. I can sense a wave of heat coming off the invisible perimeter wall, something I've never felt before.

"Where were you?" he asks, without taking his eyes off his targets.

"It doesn't matter. How long have you been here?"

"Maybe an hour. They keep coming. We'll eventually run out of power for the weapons. And for the wall, too."

We're not supposed to be talking, but who cares now?

"I'm sorry to ask this, but can you tell me where you've been sending all those DMs this month?"

Bertrand stops firing for a moment and looks at me in shock. "How did you know about that?"

"It doesn't matter. And you don't have to answer if you

don't want." I'm tired of secrets kept and secrets revealed. I need to know which side everyone is on. I need to be reassured that there are still clear sides.

"Of course I can tell you," Bertrand says. "My brother. He lives in Toronto, with our mother. She's dying. I wanted to send her pictures of Lizzie. She's her only grandchild. She's very proud of her."

"I'm sorry," I mumble, strangely relieved.

I turn back to resume shooting, as does Bertrand.

Suddenly a section of the wall in front of us sizzles, as if from an electrical short, and a hexagonal hole appears, outlined in a ribbon of gold. Our walls are constructed like a honeycomb, from a grid of such invisible hexagons. One of them has just failed, and the mantas are now trying to get in. Bertrand and I step back, horrified.

Bertrand immediately shoots two in succession as they squeeze through the opening. A third pushes the carcasses of the first two through the hole and manages to avoid the fusillade. It makes directly for me. We're firing, but it doesn't stop. It's huge with its wings outstretched, its eyes a hellish red, and everything darkens as I prepare for its embrace. It's about to wrap its wings around my head when a hand reaches out from behind me, grasps one of its murderous horns, and tears the creature out of the air. The darkness disappears, but I'm reeling, breathless. I see the attacker on its back, and a boot is crushing its head. I'm aware of someone else—it's Rupert—stepping between Bertrand and me to help fire at the next round of mantas swarming through the hole. And now I'm feeling myself swept off my feet by powerful arms and find myself looking up into Karyn's face.

"I will take you to the library," Karyn says. "We need to execute our plan."

"No, no, put me down!" I protest. "I must fight here!"

"You told us that the mission is our greatest priority," Rupert replies, even as he expertly dispatches one manta after another. "And that we must disobey all other orders."

"But this is me, Rupert," I say. "I order you to—"

"You have an estimated thirteen minutes to execute the plan," Rupert says over the hum of his weapon.

"But that's not enough time!" I cry.

"We have a 14 percent chance of success," Karyn says as she bears me away from the battle.

"But if I stay and fight—"

"Then you would have a 0 percent chance," she continues. "She's moving with startling speed and litheness. "And that would be stupid."

"I can't just leave!"

I look over Karyn's shoulder and see other hexagons in the perimeter wall glow gold and disappear. Soon the mantas will overwhelm our defenses and swarm in.

"You must leave," Karyn says. "We must leave. I'm rather sad, of course, since I haven't finished my graphic novel and I'd prefer—"

"Shut up and put me down!" I command her.

And she does stop. But not because I have commanded

her to do so.

We both watch a new spectacle unfold above us. As if strings attaching them to the sky had been cut, the mantas begin to fall with a great crashing sound of metal hitting metal. Once they filled the sky above Arcadia; now they are lying in the field beyond the cistern, stacked a half-dozen high everywhere, and this time they do not disappear into dew. The inner perimeter stops shimmering and giving off heat. With soft pops, new gold-rimmed hexagons begin to appear in the breaches and the perimeter wall becomes whole again.

It's as if someone has pulled the plug on the entire operation. It obviously wasn't my doing. Anuradha said that she no longer could influence her employers. Which leaves only one other person.

"Thank you, Benjamin," I say quietly.

Chapter Twenty

They have collected everything on the list I gave them. Now they're finishing up a final task they assigned themselves. I enter the library with the backpack that holds all my worldly possessions, hurriedly swept together, to find Rupert and Karyn sitting at a table in the empty main room. Karyn is drawing and Rupert watching. A thick stack of completed pages lies next to Karyn's elbow.

Rupert looks up as I approach, but she continues to draw.

"Hello, Rachel," Rupert says. "See what Karyn is doing."

I look over her shoulder. She's drawing the main room of the library, including remarkably faithful representations of Rupert and her at the table. As I watch, she employs the unerring skill of a photorealist to draw me entering the room.

"But you never even looked up!" I exclaim.

As she adds the final touches—the wrinkles on my face,

the crosshatching on the backpack—she says, "I don't have to. I have eyes in the back of my head."

Rupert helpfully indicates the studs in her ears, which I now understand to be functional, not decorative.

With a flourish, Karyn signs this last page and hands the folio to Rupert.

"It is complete," he says and flips through the pages, showing me different scenes. "Look. The battle. Karyn's capture. The rebellion and the split. The initial attacks back in 2032. And see, Rachel, here you are, right there at the beginning."

It's a picture of Anuradha and me, side by side, at the official opening ceremony for Arcadia. I hadn't even decided at that point whether to join. I was only there to see my friend, to hear her creation story. She'd been persuasive indeed. On that very day, I made my life-changing decision. I turn away so that my tears don't destroy Karyn's work.

"Should we take it with us, Rachel?" Rupert asks.

I shake my head. "Let's leave it here. In the library."

"Then we are ready to go," he says, glancing over at the knapsacks. One contains the dried food I will eat, another the necessary survival tools—micropanels, a desalination kit, the medical supplies I might need. The third contains the essential components of my lab necessary to reproduce my research results.

Arcadia has a half-dozen hovercars. Because of a shortage of spare parts, only two are kept in working order. Zoltan is giving us one of them. Since we will not likely return, it's an act of great generosity. The hovercar has enough of a charge to get us pretty close to where we need to go. At this time of year, there will be practically no sunlight at that latitude to recharge the cells. We'll probably have to hike the last fifty miles or more, to the coordinates of one of the largest methane deposits.

We don't know how long the grace period will last. Zoltan thinks that CRISPR International's global network might be up and running again in as little as forty-eight hours. The Movement has scored only a glancing blow.

I'm not worried about Arcadia. As long as I'm no longer here, CRISPR won't keep trying to break in to destroy my research. They'll be focused on one thing above all: finding and stopping me.

In the next hour, Anuradha will go before the community and confess everything. I'm glad I won't be here. I doubt she will be punished or confined. Like Karyn, she no longer maintains any connection to her employer. She has nothing left but Arcadia. She is an astronaut marooned on her planet. Perhaps they'll simply change her status from sleeper to Capture. Or perhaps they will send her into exile at the Farm, if it will have her.

The whole concept of Arcadia has changed for me, now that it turns out we were conceived as an ark, an instrument of salvation for the chosen remnant of humanity, the inner circle of the world's most powerful corporation.

What was going through my former husband's mind when he sent those messages to our children? Was he warning me of the serpent in our midst? More likely, he simply wanted to tell me that I was as wedded to illusions as he was. Julian couldn't have known about my research and its potential impact. He wasn't trying to save Arcadia or the world. Maybe he just wanted to get in one last jab at his ex-wife. On such small things does the fate of the world turn.

"Everyone who hears these words of mine and does not put them into practice is like a foolish person who builds his house on sand," Matthew said. "The rain comes down, the streams rise. The winds blow and beat against that house, and it falls with a great crash."

We built Arcadia on sand, and I no longer want any part of it. I don't know if it can ever rid itself of this original sin.

The plan I sketched out for Rupert and Karyn was for them to trek alone to the Arctic Circle and what remains of the polar ice cap. They were to start a carefully controlled process of ice-crystal formation. To program it for precise homeostatic growth. To provide the coordinates to Benjamin and Zoltan to shield the location from CRISPR. The mission, I thought, didn't need an eighty-year-old woman to slow it down.

But soon thereafter I changed my mind: I'm going with them. I'm not sure what I can add to Rupert's analytical abilities or Karyn's fine motor skills. Perhaps just an all-too-human sense of urgency and adventure. I'll also be there just in case Karyn starts to hit her head or Rupert needs his monkey patched. They aren't infallible, our AIs—but then, who is?

At the end of my life, I will be going on the Arctic expedition of my dreams. The ice has given me so much over the fourscore span of my life. It's time to give something back to the ice.

This report is all I have to leave behind for my three children and two grandchildren. I want them to understand my decision. I want them to know that I'm taking them with me, not by way of VR technology but in the hopes for their future that I carry in my scarred, rundown heart.

Rupert and Karyn have shouldered the bags and are watching me compose these final lines. I don't know if we can save the world.

But if I have to, I will die trying.

Chapter Twenty-One

Transcript of conversation between Emmanuel Puig and Aurora West-Sackville, Brussels, December 31, 2051

Emmanuel Puig: I know you're busy, but thank you for agreeing to meet with me. Well, virtually.

Aurora West-Sackville: I really don't have much time.

Emmanuel: I just wanted to know if you'd heard anything from your mother and her trip to... the frostlands.

Aurora: Nothing.

Emmanuel: And Arcadia?

Aurora: They're not saying anything.

Emmanuel: I suppose we'll just have to wait.

Aurora: Yes.

Emmanuel: I want to publish your mother's manuscript. The one she sent to you and you sent to me. Well, the redacted version, anyway. We don't want to reveal any of the—

Aurora: You don't have to ask my permission. It's what she would have wanted.

Emmanuel: I plan to publish your father's manuscript, too, of course, but I'm still working on the annotations.

Aurora: The work of an academic is never done.

Emmanuel: And then...

Aurora: Then what?

Emmanuel: Actually, I was thinking of a trilogy.

Aurora: Go ahead. Knock yourself out.

Emmanuel: I'm sorry?

Aurora: Oh, it's just an old expression. It means do whatever you want to do.

Emmanuel: I was thinking of something from your point of view.

Aurora: I have nothing to add and I don't have any time, so—

Emmanuel: But you'll at least think about it?

Aurora: You're serious.

Emmanuel: I am always serious.

Aurora: My father died last year. I have no idea if my mother is still alive. I don't think of myself as a paranoid person, but I have good reason to believe that the most powerful corporation in the world considers my family public enemy number one. Oh, and meanwhile, the planet is being frog-marched toward apocalypse. And you want me to write a book?

Emmanuel: A short one, perhaps.

Aurora: A book!

Emmanuel: Well, it's what we do, isn't it?

Aurora: That's the stupidest thing you've said so far.

Emmanuel: I apologize.

Aurora: We have to do more than just write books.

Emmanuel: If we can.

Aurora: I don't know about you, but I plan to do something. I'm not just going to sit around and wait.

Emmanuel: Good!

Aurora: Even if it's just a small thing, I'm going to do it. We can't let ourselves wallow in dystopia.

Emmanuel: I'm so happy to hear this!

Aurora: Enough is enough!

Emmanuel: Knock yourself out, Aurora!

Aurora: That's not exactly how you... Never mind. I have to go. We're hosting a New Year's Eve party.

Emmanuel: Of course. Then we agree?

Aurora: About what?

Emmanuel: To do something, something together.

Aurora: Together?

Emmanuel: You will write the third book in the series and I will edit it?

Aurora: Look, I really have to go...

Emmanuel: We all want to know if your mother will be successful. Perhaps you can interview her when she gets back and—

Aurora: You're irrepressibly optimistic.

Emmanuel: And I want to hear your story. The story of the next generation.

Aurora: The guests will be arriving any minute. I have to focus on the here and now before I can think about future books.

Emmanuel: Ah, but you will think about it. Thank you, Aurora, I look forward to our collaboration! I am very excited about the new year and our new project. For now, however, let us both go knock ourselves out.

Acknowledgments

This book owes its existence to Tom Engelhardt, who inspired me to write *Splinterlands* and encouraged me to continue the story in *Frostlands*. He continues to be an editor without parallel who did much to improve the text. A shoutout as well to Sarah Grey, a superb copyeditor, and the crew at Haymarket for their design and promotional skills. Finally, my wife Karin helped early on to make this a more interesting book: she remains my first reader, my dear reader, my ideal reader.

About the Author

John Feffer is a playwright and the author of several books, including *Splinterlands* and the novel *Foamers*. His articles have appeared in the *New York Times*, the *Washington Post*, the *Nation*, *Salon*, and others. He is the director of Foreign Policy in Focus at the Institute for Policy Studies.

CPSIA information can be obtained
at www.ICGtesting.com
Printed in the USA
BVHW040834010219
539250BV00004B/108/P

9 781608 465040